HAUNTED WHISPERS

A HORROR ANTHOLOGY

JOSEPH MULAK

CONTENTS

To my family for love, support, and encouragement, which may come to an end if any of you read this book.

INTRODUCTION

The book you hold in your hands is what Haunted Whispers should have been from the beginning. Unfortunately, that wasn't possible when this collection of short stories came into existence back in 2012.

At the time, I was young and had a few stories published. I had a few others sitting on my hard drive that were unpublished, probably for good reason. I decided it was time to put a book out, but the thought of writing a novel-length work seemed like a daunting task for which I wasn't quite ready. A short story collection seemed more reasonable. So, I took the stories I had already written and wrote a few more to make the book a bit thicker and set about learning how to self-publish a book since I didn't have the confidence in myself to believe a publisher would give it the time of day.

At the time, there was another author I had as a friend on Facebook who had self-published his own book. I decided to approach him and ask him how he went about it. By this time, Amazon's Createspace had been around for about twelve years, but I'd never heard of it. It seemed like an author's dream. No upfront costs. They just took a percentage of every book sold. With Createspace, I could make a print book and do an ebook with KDP. The only cost involved was the cover since a member of a writing group I was involved in a few years before was doing some work as an editor for a publisher, so he was kind of enough to help me with editing the book. Within a few months, the book was published and ready for sale.

The problem? Almost nobody bought it. A few of my co-workers purchased some copies directly from me. A couple of family members as well. Other than that, I don't recall the book getting a single sale.

This was my fault. While I was spending time learning how to self-publish a book, it never even occurred to me to learn how to market it. I had no idea how to promote myself or my work.

So, the book remained for sale, even though no one was buying it, and I busied myself writing a novel. This time, I was determined to get it published by an actual publisher. I had become disillusioned with self-publishing and I wasn't even close to ready to trying it again.

In 2014, I completed a novel called Flushed which is and probably will always be my one published work outside the horror genre. Horror is my passion but that book needed to be written. It was a form of therapy to help me through some tough times I'd been having. My first thought was to send it to an agent and hope for the best. But, another writer friend had put out a few books with a small publisher who was just starting out. At this point, they had been around for about two years. I asked my friend about her experiences with the publisher and she had nothing but nice things to say about her experience, so I sent them my manuscript. At that time, the publisher was known as Creativia but they have since rebranded as Next Chapter Publications, a much better name in my humble opinion.

Now, usually, when you send a manuscript to a publisher, a typical wait time for a response is anywhere from six months to a year. So imagine my surprise when I heard back within a week. They had a few questions for me about why I wanted to publish with them rather than self-publish, to which I responded by telling them about my lack of knowledge with regards to marketing and promotion. They told me they could help me with this and sent me a contract, which I read and signed. They worked quickly and the book was out within a few months.

I got to work on my next book, a horror novel originally called Burnt Ashes (yes, I know what horrible title it is), which is now Ashes to Ashes. The publisher of my first book picked this one up as well.

Within a few months of that one coming out, I was contacted by the publisher. They noticed I had self-published a collection of short stories and wanted to know if they could put it out under their banner. I was more than happy to oblige. The book got a complete overhaul. The publisher and I re-edited the book, they slapped a new cover on it, and I had now had three books published with them. Life seemed good.

But it wasn't. Not entirely. Haunted Whispers weighed on me for years afterward. There were some good stories in it. Stories I was proud to have written and readers seemed to enjoy. There were others, well...let's just say I wasn't *as* proud of those. Two of the stories, Home for the Holidays and Consumed, were written for specific anthologies and both were rejected. I was too naïve to realize that perhaps there were good reasons why they were turned down. Also, I was always bothered by the violence in Home for the Holidays. The story was written for an anthology of extreme horror. Now, I do enjoy reading some authors who write some pretty extreme stuff, but it was never something I enjoyed writing. I've written three extreme horror stories, one of which was published. But looking back, I'm embarrassed by all of them. Another story, The Lost, was weak. It was a good idea when I wrote, but the execution of it was lacking. It was a story written specifically for the collection and looking back on it, I should have scrapped it. A Tad Bit Ghostly is a story I enjoyed writing and some readers have said it's their favorite in the book. But it didn't fit the tone. The book was filled with haunting stories, most of which did not have a happy ending, and there's this screwball comedy at the end.

So, what was I going to do with this book in which I had no faith and could no longer claim I was proud of? I planned to pull the book from the publisher, give it a new title and cover, and pull the four previously mentioned stories and replace them with better ones written since the original publication of the book. I was going to self-publish it (yes, even though I had sworn off self-publishing for good. Trust me, I wasn't happy about it). While discussing the idea of pulling the book and me getting the publishing rights back with Next Chapter, they said they were open to the idea of me swapping out some of the stories, adding this introduction, and adding in story notes at the end of the book. The compromise was, the cover would remain (which I'm okay with, I do love the cover), as would the original title. I could live with that, especially if it meant not having to venture into the scary world of self-publishing again. I've done it twice and fell flat on my face both times.

So, dear reader, here is the new version of this book. My preferred version. I think it's a stronger book having made some changes to it and I hope you think so too.

--Joseph Mulak
Spring 2021

IN THE HANDS OF AN ANGRY GOD

THERE ARE JUST A FEW OF US LEFT NOW. AS FAR AS I know, anyway. We're so far away from civilization there could be millions of survivors still out there, but I doubt it. Things were bad when I left the city. I can't imagine they got any better.

There used to be eighteen of us. Just a collection of people who managed to stumble on the same remote cabin over the last few months. Seven of us have managed to stay alive up until now.

Bryce is still with us. Dammit. That self-absorbed pretty boy never ceases to aggravate me. Even now I can't look at him without feeling like I'm going to throw up. But he hasn't killed himself yet. I guess that's something I can say for him. I thought he would have now that he doesn't have his looks to get by anymore.

Even the women in our group, the ones that fawned over Bryce's handsome face and toned body, deny it now. They want to be seen as strong, independent, feminist women. In reality, they're the exact opposite of what they pretend to be.

Cass is the worst of them. If she could talk, nothing intelligent would come out of her mouth and

I'm sure she'd use the word "like" more often than is necessary for every sentence. I've never been so grateful for the silence. I mean, she still draws her eyebrows on. Who's she trying to impress? Not Bryce. Not anymore.

Roxanne is the one person I can stand these days. Curtis used to be okay, but he's become paranoid since Brad committed suicide. I can't say I blame him. No one ever came out and said it, but I'm pretty sure they were a couple. Or at least sleeping together. I don't know that for sure, but the way they acted around each other, they just seemed close.

But Roxanne, now there's a woman with a good head on her shoulders. She can keep calm in any situation, and she didn't show the least bit of interest in the pretty boy. Maybe that's why I like her so much. In a platonic way, mind you.

The cabin is large enough for all of us. It was cramped at first, but since the herd's been thinned out a bit, it's a lot better. There are three bedrooms. I share a room with Curtis. Roxanne and Cass have a room together, as do Camille and Autumn. Bryce is on the couch. Before, when we more than doubled our current population, people were sleeping in chairs, on the floor, wherever we could find the space. I wouldn't say I'm happy about the eleven people who killed themselves, but it is nice to sleep in a bed.

Curtis and I are in the living room. I have no idea where the others are. Maybe out for a walk in the woods. Maybe hunting for food. Maybe in another room in the house. Maybe dead. Who knows? I haven't seen any of them all day.

I'm reading. The cabin came stocked with lots of reading material, otherwise, I would have gone nuts a long time ago and checked out like the others. Curtis is sitting in the chair across from me. When I look up, he's writing on his notepad. It's the little things I miss. Like the sound of a pencil scratching on the paper. You don't notice these things until they're gone. He tears out the sheet and hands it to me.

"Do you think this will ever end?" it asks me.

I shrug. No sense in writing something I can convey with a gesture. Paper is running low and I have no idea if we'll be getting more any time soon. I'm thinking at some point we'll have to find a way into town to get some supplies. Assuming there are any left. After a year, who knows how much has already been looted.

I hand the sheet back to Curtis and he starts writing something else on it before giving it back. "I miss Brad."

I write, "I know." And give it back.

"I miss the others too."

I nod. I get the impression Curtis is like me in that he has very little respect for those who are left. He spends a lot of time with Roxanne, but he tends to avoid the rest of them as I do.

He doesn't write anything else, so I assume the conversation is over and go back to my book. The pickings are slim these days. I've already burned through the thrillers and mysteries and I'm reading the classics now. War and Peace. I figured it should last a while but I'm not enjoying it. It's dry and long-winded, but it's a time killer.

I can feel Curtis' eyes on me, and when I look up he's staring at me, pleading. I don't know what to do. He's upset, I can see that. He's alone and depressed and I have no way of comforting him. We're screwed. That's all there is to it.

But he won't stop looking at me and it's distracting. I have no idea what the hell he wants from me. Hell, I could use some comforting myself. Curtis isn't the only one who has lost people. I had a family once. Back before all this started. I had a wife and an unborn child.

Now they're gone and here I am with a bunch of strangers, most of whom I don't even like. Funny how things work out.

Camille and Autumn walk into the room, startling me. I don't hear their footsteps approaching. Of course I don't. I haven't heard anything in over a year. They're both crying and I know before they can show us. I know we lost someone else.

The girls lead us outside to the back of the cabin where Roxanne had found a shotgun and killed herself.

Dammit. I was hoping it was Bryce.

But I can't say I'm surprised. I can't blame her. I think about doing the same thing every minute of every day. I don't know what keeps me from going through with it.

I motion for the girls to go back into the house. Curtis and I grab shovels and start digging a hole. I can tell he doesn't want to. He's upset and shaking from holding back tears, but I don't want to do this alone. I'm holding back tears too, but I hide it better.

It's a difficult task. Not just the actual labor. But burying a body--a *human being*--never gets easier. I'm sure that someday I'll be doing this for Curtis. And then I will cry.

We finish packing the dirt. I lean on my shovel and

wipe the sweat from my forehead. I want to say something. Words of encouragement or my favorite memory of Roxanne. Something. But I can't. I can only *think* what I want to say. Writing it wouldn't have the same effect as if I'd said it out loud.

I go back into the house, but Curtis stays behind, staring at the spot where we buried our friend. I leave him to his grief.

The girls are in the living room, seated where Curtis and I had been earlier, both still crying.

Autumn takes out her notepad. Hers has a lot more blank pages than mine. She's not much of a talker.

"Why is He doing this to us?" she writes, and I shrug. I ask myself that same question every waking moment and I have yet to come up with an answer. I don't even have so much as a theory.

I wait for a follow-up question, but there isn't one. We already know *who* is doing this. We just don't know *why*.

I find an empty chair and sit. We all just stare at each other, trying to make sense of what our lives have become, why we choose to keep going on. But it's a useless endeavor.

We stay there until the sun goes down. Curtis hasn't returned and there's still no sign of Bryce. I think about going outside to look for Curtis but I'm afraid of what I might find. Maybe Roxanne's death was too much for him. The straw that broke the camel's back, so to speak. I can't take too much heartache in one day. If Curtis is dead, he can wait until morning.

I don't care where Bryce is. I don't want to see him, and I hope he's either dead or run away in search of something better. Maybe that makes me a bad person, but I don't care anymore. Think of me what you will. I am who I am.

I start to feel tired and leave the room. I go to my bed and lie down since there's nothing else to do. I spend a lot of my time sleeping. Or, at least, lying in bed trying to sleep. With everything going on, it's hard. I toss and turn, unable to get comfortable.

Tonight is no different. I keep seeing Roxanne's lifeless eye staring at me. Just the one since half her face was missing from the scatter of the pellets. I can't get the image out of my head. I see it every time I close my eyes, so I keep them opened and I stare at the wall, hoping sleep will find me.

I feel someone in the room with me. I assume it's Curtis coming back, but when I prop myself up on my elbow to look, it's Autumn. She stands in the doorway for a few moments, as if trying to decide on something.

She walks over, slowly, and sits down on my bed, stroking my back.

I'm uncomfortable, but I can't say anything.

She kisses my neck several times and I remember the first time I made love to Amber after the world was taken over by the silence. It wasn't the same not even close. I couldn't hear the sound of our bodies slamming together, her moans, her calling out my name.

It seemed empty.

I never touched her again after that.

When I found her dead in our basement, hanging from the ceiling, I thought it was my fault. I still do.

I can feel Autumn's touch as she places her hands under my shirt but can't hear the smack of her lips as she lifts it and kisses my chest.

Maybe that's why I put my hands on her shoulders and push her away.

Or maybe it's because I still have the image of Roxanne stuck in my head and it dampens the mood.

Or even because I know she's looking for comfort and would seek it with any available man and I just happen to be there. But I know she would rather Bryce as he used to be, but she can't have that now. Not ever again.

Whatever the reason, I stop her. She looks at me for a long moment, confused, trying to figure out if I'm serious.

Even I'm surprised. I'd be lying if I said I never looked at her with lust, sneaking quick glances at her thin body when I thought she wasn't looking. Staring at her ass when she wore short shorts and the tight shirts that hugged her body and showed off her perfect breasts. I'd fantasized about this moment more often than I care to admit, but I just can't go through with it. I know it wouldn't be right.

She leaves the room and I'm left to wonder if it happened or if I'd imagined the whole thing.

In the morning, when I see her, neither of us can look the other in the eye. I'm searching through the cupboards looking for something to eat. It's been a few days since I've had anything. I'll have to go hunting later since we're out of canned provisions. I don't think we're too far away from the nearest town. Maybe I can go for a walk later and find a store that hasn't been picked clean.

Autumn comes up behind me and sticks a note in my face.

"Did Curtis come back last night?"

I shake my head and write my own note. "If he did,

he got up before me. He wasn't in his bed when I woke up."

She looks worried. She likes Curtis. We all do. There's a childlike innocence we found refreshing. I'm worried too.

"I'm sure he's fine," I write. "I'll go look for him in a bit."

She gives me a solemn nod and I can tell she's not comforted, but there's not much more I can do for her.

Bryce walks into the kitchen and I lose my appetite. That face. It makes me want to throw up every time I see it.

Autumn leaves as soon as he walks in and I see the hurt in his eyes. He knows it's because of him, but he has no control over it. I won't go so far as to say it's not his fault. It is. It was his own stupidity.

It was a few months back. There were more of us then. Fourteen, I think. One of our ranks was a fanatical religious woman. Nancy. An older lady. She was a little weird, but nice. The others made fun of her because she spent most of her time reading the Bible. Notes were passed between us, making fun of her and inquiring how she could still believe in God after what had happened. I tried not to make fun of her. I didn't see anything wrong with having faith in something that gives you hope. She wasn't hurting anybody by reading the Bible and praying. She was just trying to find some peace among the chaos, like the rest of us.

We were sitting in the cabin's living room. All of us. Passing notes back and forth, offering ideas as to what was going on. Nancy had dared to offer her opinion.

"God is punishing the world," she wrote. "Just as he had in the days of Noah." The note was passed around. Most people glanced at it, realized it was just more of her religious gibberish, and passed it along to the next person without giving it another thought.

Until the note reached Bryce.

He read it, the disdain showing on his face. He didn't pass the note. Instead, he stood up and walked out of the room, returning with a sheet of paper and a black marker. On it, he had written "FUCK GOD" and slammed the paper on the coffee table for everyone to see.

That's when Nancy ran out of the room.

We all assumed she was hurt by what Bryce did and needed a few moments to regain her composure, so we didn't think anything of it. I can't speak for anyone else, but I thought that Bryce had crossed a line and what he did was unnecessary and cruel. But he didn't deserve what he got.

What none of us had suspected was that Nancy had gone to the kitchen. Because of the silence, none of us could hear what she was doing.

She returned with a large knife and before any of us could react, she pounced on Bryce, slashing at him in anger. No thought behind it, just slashing blindly, hoping to hit something.

She got his face several times. He put his hands up to protect himself and got his arm sliced up pretty good.

It was the first time I'd seen someone in pain, screaming and begging for help without a sound. It was a surreal moment.

We rushed to his aid. If I'm being honest, I did it because I knew I would be judged afterward if I didn't at least pretend to help. We managed to pull her off, but not before the damage had been done. Bryce's face had been cut up beyond recognition.

Camille was a nurse. She grabbed the first aid kit and patched him up as best she could, but without the benefit of a hospital and the proper equipment, she was limited in what she could do.

Nancy continued to fight us, still trying to go after Bryce, which left us with the unpleasant task of figuring out what to do with her.

In the end, there was one option. We couldn't trust her. Kicking her out wasn't even viable since we had no idea if she might try to come back, this time wanting to kill more than just Bryce.

No. Death was the only way to ensure the safety of everyone else in the cabin. We hung her outside, behind the house. None of us knew how to tie a proper noose, so we stood there watching her struggle as she choked to death. It took a lot longer than I expected and I took no pleasure in watching her die. Hell, I wish she had finished the job on Bryce at least. But instead of killing him, she left him disfigured, the scars making his face look like ground beef. A fate worse than death, for Bryce and for us since we're the ones who have to look at him.

If he hadn't decided to be a jerk, he'd still have his looks and his pick of the women who are left. Poetic justice if you ask me. He insulted what she loves most, God, so she took away what he loves most, his looks.

So, Bryce hands me a note. "I found Curtis."

As difficult as it is, I look at his face, searching for some sign that it was good news. He shook his head.

Dammit. Another body to bury.

Five of us left now.

I scrawl a quick note and hand it to him. "Don't tell the girls about this." He nods and I run out the door to bury the body before anyone else can find it.

I realize how dumb this is before I even get there. There's no way I can bury Curtis that quick. Even with the two of us, it took over an hour to get Roxanne into the ground. By myself, it would take even longer.

I decide to drag Curtis into the woods and hide the body until everyone is asleep and I have more time.

I'm not going to tell you how he did it. It's too gruesome. It was almost as if he felt he needed to punish himself for something he had done and so made his own death as painful as possible.

I hide the body and hope no one asks me if I've seen Curtis. I don't want to lie but I'm doing my best to keep people alive.

I'm just not doing a very good job of it.

There's a river near the house where I clean up. My shirt is full of blood, so I take it off and leave it with Curtis' body. I managed to keep my pants clean, which is good. I can get away with going around with no shirt on. It would be embarrassing to have to explain why I'm walking around with no pants.

I go back to the house but I don't see anyone at first. It seems like everyone needs to be alone to mourn. I can't blame them. We all liked Roxanne. She had an upbeat personality that you couldn't help but like. It was going to take some time for all of us to recover.

I sit down on the couch in the living room. I don't bother trying to read. I know I won't be able to concentrate on a book right now. Instead, I just sit, trying to clear my mind of all the shit that's happened in the last little while, and find some peace.

Of course, this doesn't happen. Trying to force it all out of my head just brings it back up and makes me think of it even more. God, too much has happened in such a short time. Less than a year and a half ago I was married, expecting my first child, had a great career. Now, look at the way things are. The five of us could be the last people on Earth for all I know.

Autumn was the last person to arrive and she's been here for at least eight months.

I think.

It's hard to keep track of time these days, but I'm pretty sure it's been eight or nine months.

I don't know if that means anything, but the last time I was anywhere near civilization, it didn't look too hopeful.

When things went quiet, people panicked. Most of us thought we had gone deaf. It was like God had pointed a remote control at the world and hit the mute button.

It wasn't until we realized that everyone else was going through the same thing that we figured out we had it wrong. *We* didn't go deaf. *Everything else* went quiet. We had no idea why. In just one minute everything was fine. The next, no birds chirping, no scraping of shoes on the sidewalk, no wind rustling through the leaves, no dogs barking. Nothing.

So yeah, people panicked. But we got back into the groove. It was weird, but you know, if we, as a society, can band together, we can stick it out. After all, we still had electricity, running water. Even our cell phones still worked. We could text to communicate. We even had internet still, so email and instant messaging were great ways to keep communication alive too. We were set.

And it worked out great. That is until the cell phones and the internet stopped working. That's when all hell broke loose. No one could stand to live in a world without electronic communication.

People turned feral, attacking others for no reason. People either committed suicide or were killed by some raving lunatic.

It was weird that electronics were holding the fabric of society together. I mean, I always knew cell phones and social media were important to people, but this important? Not even I would have guessed it.

Amber and I hid in our home for as long as we could, but our supplies were low and I was going to have to go out in search of more soon. She begged me not to. She said she didn't know what she would do if anything happened to me.

I tried to be the voice of reason and told her that we would both die, not to mention our unborn child, if I didn't go. She gave up trying to convince me.

The next day I left. I was only gone a few hours. I had managed to grab a few things. A couple of days' worth of food, nothing much. Turns out it was all for nothing. When I got back, that's when I found her hanging in the basement. She had left a note saying she didn't want to raise our child in this world after what it had become.

After that, I didn't see the point in sticking around.

That's when I left and stumbled upon the cabin. There were already nine people there. Somehow we all happened to stumble upon it in the middle of nowhere. The rule of the house is that no one is turned away. Anyone who needs help, food, or shelter gets it. That's how we ended up with eighteen people under the roof at one time.

I see something moving off to the side. When I turn my head, I see Bryce entering the room. He's pale.

He looks like he's about to throw up. Tears are welling up in his eyes.

My first thought is another suicide and I know my heart can't take yet another. I just finished burying Curtis, I don't want to have to bury someone else so soon.

But then I notice the knife in his hand, fresh blood still dripping from the blade.

What did you do? I mouth the words slowly so he won't misunderstand. *What the hell did you do?*

He stares at me for a few seconds and I think he's formulating a response. But before I get one, he drops the knife and bolts for the door. Every instinct tells me to go after him and beat him until my knuckles bleed, but the knife and the blood worry me and I have to see what happened.

I check the bedrooms. Mine is empty, of course. I shared it with Curtis and he's gone now. When I check the next room, I find them. Camille, Cass, and Autumn. All dead, their throats slit. The kills are fresh. A few spurts of blood spew from Autumn's neck before stopping.

I can't believe it. As much as I hate Bryce, as selfish as he is, I never thought him capable of something like this. I'm sure the girls didn't see it coming either. Or heard it.

I drop to my knees, tears pouring from my eyes. I may not have liked them, but never would I have wished anything like this on any of them. But in a way, I envied them and the others that have gone before me. Their suffering is at an end while mine continues. I don't have the guts to end it like so many before me.

Maybe that's what Bryce was trying to do. End their suffering.

I think about going after him, but I have no idea which way he went. I have no wish to stumble around hoping to find him.

Instead, I stand up and go back to the living room. Back to the couch.

I don't know what to do. I am alone for the first time in over a year and I have no idea what to do or where to go.

Why? Why is this happening? I think. It's almost a prayer but not quite. I was never a spiritual person.

"You did this to yourselves."

It's a voice. An honest-to-god voice. I hear it. It's not my imagination.

I look around, trying to see whoever is speaking. But I'm alone.

I try to call out, hoping that the silence is gone, but nothing comes out. I try again but get the same result.

"Don't bother. The silence has not been lifted. You can hear me because I am the cause of it and thus I am outside of it."

Who are you? I figure if it heard my thoughts the first time, it could do it again. God?

"Some call me that, but I have many names."

Why are you doing this?

"As I said, this is your own doing. I didn't destroy you. You destroyed yourselves, as I knew you would."

But why? Why did you create the silence?

"What other choice did I have? Would anyone want to see their creation spew hatred from their mouths at every turn? You were not meant for this. I created you to be kind and loving toward one another. But you rejected that and you used words to hurt one another, to lie, to harm reputations, to bully, to cause others to take their own lives out of shame or because they could not take it anymore. I've watched this go on for centuries and I could bear it no more."

Oh my god, I'm going crazy. My mind has snapped, and I think God is talking to me.

"I had hoped that without communication, you would see the error of your ways, but in my heart, I knew it wouldn't change anything. I am sad to say I was right."

So what now?

"What now? Nothing. You will do whatever it is you decided to do. The human race will die out and there will be nothing left. As for me, I will go on existing as I always have."

You're not going to create a new race?

"No. I have learned my lesson. I cannot create a race with freewill and expect them to love one another. It's not possible. And to create a race of mindless robots would be meaningless. Once all humanity is dead, your race will become extinct."

Am I the last?

"There are still many left, spread out across the Earth. I have been watching them as I have watched you. They're no better off. They will be dead soon as well."

I'm not convinced that extinction is inevitable. What if people have children? And those children learn to survive as well? We could start over."

Maybe we will survive. Maybe we'll surprise you.

"I doubt that. I have been here since before the dawn of time. I created your race and have been watching it ever since. Nothing you do surprises me. You are predictable. You have a tendency toward violence that angers me, and I will ensure your destruction. There is nothing to be done about it. I should have seen this coming sooner."

I stand up. I'm not about to give up just because God tells me there's no hope. I know there are still people left. I just need to find them.

I start to search the cabin for supplies. There's nothing left for me at the cabin now. I need to move on.

When I find other survivors, we will work to rebuild our race and the humans will have dominion over the Earth once again.

Even though we are in the hands of an angry god, we will survive in defiance of the loving father who turned his back on us.

TERROR EYES

AT THE TOP OF THE STAIRS, TED PAUSED TO CATCH HIS breath, huffing and wheezing thanks to fifteen years of smoking, and listened for another scream.

He walked to the first door on the left where he could hear a quiet sob coming from the other side, which surprised him since Serena seldom woke in the middle of the night. Not since she was a baby.

He slowly turned the knob and pushed the door as quietly as he could, but it still made a slight creak. The only light came from the hallway, and he could barely define the outline of his daughter sitting up in her bed, the covers pulled up to her chin.

He stepped into the room and immediately felt a chill run through his entire body. He crossed the room to the window and silently cursed his wife, Amy, for leaving it ajar after tucking Serena in for the night.

There had been a time when Serena's bedtime was a family affair. Father, mother, and daughter would sit on the bed. They would read Serena a bedtime story and sing a few songs with her. Then, at Amy's insistence, they would lead Serena in prayer before kissing Serena goodnight. Once she was tucked in, Ted and

Amy would go back downstairs for their alone time together.

They hadn't done this in almost a year, yet Amy still insisted on saying a prayer every night.

Ted, who was not the least bit religious, like his wife claimed to be, only read the story and sang a few songs with her.

When he reached the window, Ted found that it was already closed. He put his hand up to it and felt around the sides trying to find where the draft was coming in, but there was nothing. Then, remembering his daughter, who still sobbed on the bed, he forgot about the window and walked over to her. He placed his hand on her shoulder, noticing she was incredibly warm.

"What's the matter, Princess?"

She said something through her tears, but Ted couldn't manage to decipher it.

"Okay," he said. "Stop crying, Sweetie. Then tell me what's wrong."

Serena tried to force herself to hold back the tears and speak clearly. Finally, when the tears had been choked back, she said, "I don't like the man in my room."

"But, I'm the man in your room. You don't like me?"

She managed a smile at him. "No. The other man."

Ted looked around the room. "Honey, there's no one here but you and me."

"Uh-huh. There's a man in the closet."

"In the closet?"

She nodded.

"What does he look like?"

"He's tall and has a big hat and a big black coat." Then, as an afterthought, "And he was on fire."

Ted had to bite his lip to keep from laughing. He hoped Serena didn't notice. "On fire?"

She nodded.

"Was he screaming?"

"Uh-uh."

"You'd think he'd scream if he was on fire."

"No, he just talked to me."

"What did he say?"

"He asked where Mommy was."

"And what did you tell him?"

"I told him I didn't know."

Ted waited while she sat there, as if thinking about something for a second then asked,

"Where is Mommy?"

The question made Ted bitter for a moment. It took him a moment to find a way to answer the question. His first thought was she was out screwing some other guy. He realized that was probably not the best response to give her, joking or not, he responded, "Mommy went out for a while. "I think you had a bad dream, sweetie."

"Uh-uh. I was awake."

"And why were you awake? You're supposed to be sleeping."

"The man woke me up."

"And he's in the closet right now?"

"Yes."

Ted stood up and approached the closet. He grabbed the handle and looked over at his daughter who now had the blanket pulled over her head. He yanked open the door and looked inside.

"Oh my god!" Ted screamed, and Serena poked

her head out a little. "This closet is a mess. If there was someone in here, I wouldn't be able to find him."

Serena chuckled.

Ted moved a few things around. "I don't think there's anybody in here."

"Where did he go?"

"Back into your imagination."

"He was there," she insisted.

"No one can get into your room, honey."

"How come?"

"Because if they tried, I'd tickle them." Then to prove his point, Ted jumped on the bed and tickled Serena's sides.

"Okay, time to go back to bed," he told her when she was done laughing. "Goodnight."

"Read me a story."

"No. It's time for you to go to sleep."

"Story!"

"Serena, go to sleep."

She was about to protest once more but thought better of it. Instead, she pouted and quickly rolled over to go to sleep.

Once back downstairs, Ted lay on the couch and resumed watching his movie. Whenever Amy was out, he took advantage of the situation by watching a horror movie since she normally wouldn't allow him to watch them in the house. Amy once told him it allowed evil spirits to enter their home. Even though Ted knew it was a crock, he had stopped watch horror films when she was around, just because he got sick of the nagging.

He checked his watch. It was one-thirty in the morning. Amy had left at nine o'clock, saying she was going to the movies with some friends. But Ted knew exactly where she was.

His bitter thoughts distracted his attention from the movie. Thinking about his wife led to thoughts about quick rep of about her in bed with Brian. He got a visual image in his mind of her on top of her lover, and him with his hands going up and down her body as they made love. With every second, his hatred for them grew.

Then, he threw himself into the image. Standing over them with a knife in his hand. He walked up behind Amy and grabbed her by the hair while she was still riding her lover. He saw the horrified look on Brian's face as he placed the knife to her throat and began to cut. Brian didn't budge, not even to pull out of Amy. It was as if he were too afraid to move. He laid there underneath her, frozen by fear, letting the blood from her throat pour down her body onto his.

Finally, still holding her by the hair, Ted threw her corpse to the floor and began advancing toward Brian, the knife still in his right hand, held up to make sure Brian saw it and knew what he was going to do with it.

Just as he lowered the knife toward Brian's naked and vulnerable flesh, Amy walked in the front door, interrupting his fantasy.

She was being quiet, obviously thinking Ted was still asleep. Then she walked into the living room. "You're still awake?" she said casually.

"Yeah." He took a glance at his watch. It was now quarter after two. "How was the movie?"

"Not bad." She left it at that and went to the kitchen. He could hear her pouring herself a glass of something from the fridge.

"How's Brian?" he called out while she was still in the kitchen. She emerged a moment later.

"What?"

"Nothing." He was tempted to go on, hoping to get her to confess her indiscretion, but decided he didn't feel like an argument. "What was the name of the movie?"

"Can't remember the title."

Amy gulped down the rest of her juice. "How was Serena?"

"Alright. She woke from a nightmare a little while ago. But she's okay now."

"A nightmare?"

"Yeah, she thought a man was hiding in her closet."

Amy nodded. "I'll make sure she's okay."

"Good idea," Ted said bitterly. "Because we all know I'm completely inept as a father. Totally incapable of handling something as simple as our child having a nightmare."

Amy just shrugged. "Okay, I'm off to bed."

"Okay," he said, turning his attention back to the TV.

"Goodnight."

"Bye."

Amy took off her makeup and put on her nightgown then went into Serena's room. She slept with her daughter so that Ted could have the bed. He would normally fall asleep on the couch, but would inevitably wake up in the middle of the night and stumble upstairs. Since she no longer felt comfortable sleeping next to him, she slept in Serena's room. She also saw it as a good way to bond with her daughter.

As soon as she stepped into the room she felt

chilly, but couldn't understand why. The window was closed and the thermostat hadn't been changed. When she touched her daughter, the little girl was warm. Almost hot.

She decided to talk to Ted about it in the morning then crawled into bed, pulling the blanket over herself and curling up to get warm.

She rolled onto her side and closed her eyes, yet sleep refused to come. Every time she closed her eyes, she saw Brian. She visualized him kissing her all over her body. She remembered how it felt only a little while ago as they made love.

Then the thought came to her. What if she had gotten pregnant? She and Brian hadn't used protection. How would she explain that to her husband? Despite their marital problems, she always tried to keep up the appearance of a happy marriage around others, mostly for Serena's sake.

She'd met Brian a year before and realized marrying Ted had been a mistake. Brian was romantic and obviously cared about her. He treated her like a queen, the way Ted did when they first met back in high school. But once they got married, everything changed. Ted slowly became more and more distant. They never talked at night after Serena was in bed anymore. Instead, Ted watched TV all night. He even stopped eating at the dinner table. He chose to eat his supper on the couch while watching TV.

Brian listened to her. When they were done making love, she would pour out her marital woes out to him, and he listened intently and always said the right thing to comfort her. When she was done, he would always tell her she should leave Ted, and Amy and Serena could live with him.

Deep in her heart, Amy knew he was right. She should take Serena and leave Ted. But something always held her back. Perhaps she didn't want to admit she had failed at her marriage.

Her memories of her night with Brian were interrupted by a creaking sound. At first, she thought it was Ted peeking into the bedroom to check on Serena. But a glance at the door proved it was still closed. The sound had come from somewhere else in the room.

The next sound she heard was the rattling of chains. She turned her gaze to the corner of the room just in time to see a man emerge from the closet.

She could see his outline, lit up in the darkness by a blue flame that surrounded him. He was tall. He wore a wide-brimmed hat and trench coat, with chains wrapped around his body that rattled as he walked toward her.

The flames lit up the man's monstrous face. He had sharp teeth, his skin was brown and rotted, and where his nose should have been were two gaping black holes. He had huge eye sockets, both hollow.

Wanting only to grab her daughter and run, Amy found that she couldn't move, as if this creature had put some sort of spell on her, paralyzing her.

Her next thought was to scream for Ted, but fear and the realization that he probably wouldn't bother coming anyway choked it back. She stared at the creature before her, eyes wide with surprise and her heart rate rising in panic. Finally, she was able to choke out a few words.

"Wh-Who are you?"

"I am Rogziel. The Wrath of God."

"Are you a demon?"

The man shook his head. "I am an angel of the Lord."

"An angel?"

"What were you expecting? White robe? Halo? Harp?"

Amy nodded.

"Yes, I can understand why those images might have formed your opinion on what we are supposed to look like, but no one has ever seen an angel and lived to describe it. Those pictures are how man has decided we should appear."

"Why are you here?"

"For you."

Amy gulped "Me?"

"Yes. Your time has come."

Amy couldn't believe what she was hearing. "I'm going to die?"

"Yes."

"And then I'm going to heaven?"

Rogziel shook his head.

"But, I'm a Christian. I accepted Jesus in my heart."

Again, the angel shook his head. "The book you have been taught to believe was written by man. It is full of errors."

"But what about Jesus dying for our sins?"

"Jesus Christ was not the son of God. He was human. Just like you."

"No," she shook her head at him. "I don't believe you. My parents told me about Jesus. They wouldn't lie."

"Did they tell you about Santa Claus and the Easter Bunny too? Not believing it is your choice, but the truth is the truth."

"Let's pretend for a minute you're telling me the truth, why am I going to hell? I'm a good person."

"Are you? Do you believe that?"

Amy nodded.

"Where were you tonight? Who are you with almost every night when you should be with your husband and child? That's a breach of your marital vows. Big no-no with the big guy upstairs."

Amy didn't respond. She couldn't believe everything she had been taught by her parents and in church was a lie.

"Okay," Rogziel said. "It's time to go."

"Go where?"

But the angel didn't reply. Instead, he took a step toward her. When he spoke again, his voice had changed. It had become deeper, booming. Almost, malevolent. "Look into my eyes and see your fate."

She tried to resist but found that she couldn't. Something compelled her to stare into the angel's hollow sockets.

Everything around her disappeared. The bed, the dresser, and all of Serena's toys were gone. She was engulfed in darkness. Beings were flying through the void. Evil-looking creatures that looked like skeletons with wings.

Then a river came into view. It was red, as if filled with blood, and burned with bright red fire. Then, she saw people in the flames, their heads bobbing up and down in the river, flailing their arms about and screaming. Some of them screamed for God to help them. Over and over they cried out to the Lord to save them. But their screams were only met with deep, booming laughter. Laughter so evil, it sent a chill through Amy's spine.

And then a voice. It was Rogziel's.

"Welcome to your eternity," he said.

Amy felt every muscle in her body tighten as she gazed upon her fate. She held her face in her shaking hands, sobbing loudly and begging God to forgive her.

"God can't hear you anymore," Rogziel told her. "It's time."

She finally realized that he was right about everything. There was no denying it now. She saw what awaited her in eternity with her own eyes. That's when she snapped. Once again she had found the ability to move and she took advantage of it. In one quick movement, she jumped out of bed and bolted for the door. Rogziel merely pointed at it and it locked. She ran into it, landing flat on her back.

Rogziel looked down at her. "Are you done?"

She nodded submissively.

"Good."

The angel disappeared and Amy was by herself, still in Serena's room. She stood up and looked around and saw no one except her daughter, quietly sleeping beside her.

She felt something wrench in her chest and she collapsed.

That morning, a Saturday, Ted woke to the sound of a morning talk show on the TV.

He checked the time. It was after eleven. The weird thing was Amy and Serena were usually awake by now. But the house was silent.

He turned off the TV and climbed the steps to his daughter's bedroom. When he opened the door Serena was playing on the floor with her dolls. Amy was lying on her back.

He walked over to the bed and gently shook her.

When she didn't wake up, he shook her a little harder. Still nothing. It was then he noticed her eyes were open and lifeless. Ted stumbled backward, tripping over a rollerblade Serena had left on the floor. Surprised, he cried out.

"Dad," Serena said looking up at him. "You have to be quiet. Mommy's still sleeping."

Ted screamed.

QUALITY OF LIFE

The man who came into my office was upset. Of course, everyone who came to see me was. If they weren't, there'd be no reason for them to procure my services. This guy was middle-aged, a little on the short side, balding, and wore thick glasses. I got the impression he was pretty nervous when he came in. His voice was shaking as he greeted me.

"Have a seat, Mr..."

"Edwards," he said, taking the chair directly across from my desk. "Nathan Edwards."

"I got your name from my friend, Mi—"

"Won't do any good to give me his name. I'll neither confirm nor deny that I know the person. I protect the identity of all my clients. I'm sure you understand, considering the nature of my business."

"Of course."

"Good. And of course, the same will go for you as well. No one will ever know you were here."

"I appreciate that."

He seemed to relax a little, which was good. After all, my job was pretty much to provide peace of mind to my clients. I liked to think I was good at my job.

The sign on my door read "Tom Hutchens: P.I." It was only half true. I kept my business private, but there was no investigating involved at all. Since what I did wasn't exactly legal, I needed some sort of front, and P.I. was just as good as any.

"So, I need to know the situation we're dealing with."

"It's my mother..." he trailed off as tears began to form in his eyes. I waited for him to regain his composure so he could continue. This wasn't an unusual situation. Most of my clients were emotional when they came to me.

"Take your time," I told him.

"She's in one of those asylums. I couldn't look after her myself anymore. Lord knows I tried. I just...I just can't bear to see her there anymore. It isn't the place for her."

"I understand, Mr. Edwards. Your mother, is she here in town?"

He nodded, unable to speak because he was choking up again.

"And is it safe to assume her last name is the same as yours?"

Again he nodded.

"Okay then. That's all I need. The only thing left is the matter of payment."

"Yes...I....well, I came to you because I heard not only were you the best, but you did the work...humanely, and that you were also the..."

"Cheapest," I finished for him.

"Uh...yeah."

I smiled at him. PR was a big part of my job. "Mr. Edwards, I didn't get into this business for the same reason most of my competitors did. I believe in what I do, and I believe I am providing a valuable service. The fact is, I do it because it needs to be done and because it's the right thing to do." I paused for a brief moment to let that sink in. "I don't do this for the money. Hell, I'd operate for free if I could afford to, but unfortunately, one needs to make a living."

"Of course. I understand that completely. It's just that...well..."

"Money's a little tight right now."

He nodded.

"Well, I'm sure we can come to an arrangement. As you said before, I'm the cheapest around." I'd been the one to say it, I'd said it, but I didn't feel the need to split hairs. "The reason for that is because I don't believe you and your loved ones should suffer because you're not as well off as some others. It's also because, as I said, I believe in what I do. I don't think people should suffer if they don't have to.

"I appreciate that."

"So, I try to be as accommodating as I can. I'm willing to work on a payment plan, providing you can give me something up front. Not that I don't trust you, but even though I want to help you, I need to make a living."

He stared past me, as though deep in thought.

"And I only take cash."

"Umm...I can give you Two hundred cash right now."

"That'll do," I told him. "How much can you afford per month?"

"I don't know...maybe four hundred?"

"You don't sound too sure of yourself. Let's make it two-fifty. I think that might be more within your budget."

Again, he nodded. I was pretty sure he'd start bawling again if he tried to talk. This was never easy for anyone. If it was, I wouldn't be dealing with those people. I was here to ease suffering, not help get rid of those who were treated as burdens. I didn't operate that way.

He gave me the cash and left. I did my best to reassure him his mother wouldn't feel a thing, and it would be done by tomorrow night. Even though Edwards seemed calmer as he left, I knew he was second-guessing himself. Understandable. This was a grey area, and no one was ever one-hundred percent sure they had made the right decision. No amount of reassuring I did was going to change that.

I watched him leave, my heartbreaking. I knew exactly what he was going through. I knew what it was like to suffer the way he was suffering. It was hard when a loved one turned. They looked at you as if they didn't know who you are anymore. The blank stare they gave you, the occasional attacks, it got hard to deal with. Which was why the asylum seemed like a good choice at first.

It didn't take many of them long before they came to see me.

I knew the way to the asylum well enough I could have driven there with my eyes closed. Probably about ninety percent of my business was there.

I didn't necessarily enjoy my job. I mean, by definition, I suppose I was a hitman. That bothered me a lot. I never liked to think of it as killing people for money. Some people didn't. They never thought of the victims as "people" and I always figured it was to help them feel better about what they did. I couldn't rationalize that way. I think because my situation was different than most in my line of work.

The plague, as it had come to be known, started a few years ago. Scientists are still trying to figure out why it started. No one knows for sure, though everyone seems to have a theory.

All anyone knows for certain is people just started coming back from the dead one day.

And of course, the government reacted to all the brain-dead corpses walking around just like you'd have expected them to. They gave the order to shoot them on sight.

A special task force was instituted in Aspen Falls specifically to deal with this epidemic. They drove around shooting the things in the head. Most of the cops assigned to this duty loved it. They got to kill things all day. For most of them, it was heaven.

There was one cop who hated it. He did it because he was told to do it, and that was it. He would have rathered be back on the beat writing tickets if he could. Unfortunately, Zombie Duty—as it came to be known—wasn't voluntary. You just got assigned to it.

It was that cop who discovered something no one else picked up on.

It happened during one of their raids. There were more zombies than usual in the group, and the cops weren't able to dispatch them as quickly as usual. They were on the streets, firing at anything moving, and some of the zombies were getting a little closer than they'd like.

So this particular cop, when one zombie got about a foot away from him while he was shooting at another mobile corpse, turned to see this other one in his face. Instinct made bring up the butt of his shotgun—since those seemed to work best for blowing apart the head and disabling them—and rammed him in the face. The zombie stumbled backward, far enough for the officer to aim the muzzle of the shotgun at it. There was a slight moment of hesitation. Just enough for the cop to see something in his prey's eyes. Fear.

It was at that moment this cop realized something. These things weren't brain-dead after all. Something happened to them to make them appear that way, but this "thing" had felt the pain of the gun smashing into its face, and right now it was feeling fear.

Without another thought, the cop dropped his gun and walked away, unable to bring himself to kill anymore.

Of course, there were the feelings of guilt that came with the knowledge he had been killing people all this time. These feelings led the cop to start drinking and life for him went downhill from there.

It didn't take long for the media to get involved. Once it was discovered why one of the members of this task force had simply walked off the job in the middle of a raid, people began to get involved. Scientists wanted to figure out how it was zombies could appear to have no brain functions and rely only on their animal instincts, while still having cognitive thought. People also form groups to preserve the rights of zombies, since it was now evident they indeed did possess cognitive thought. These groups staged protests, demanding zombies be treated like people and given equal rights.

It being an election year, the government caved into the demands and zombie-ism became a form of mental illness.

The families of those infected did their best to care for their loved ones at home, but this rarely lasted very long. Some places opened up homes for zombies and colleges even began to offer diploma programs specifically designed to train people who were willing to work in such homes.

Other cities with mental hospitals—such as Aspen Falls—devoted a ward or two to care for the living dead.

Most people weren't happy with this turn of events. Especially the nurses who work in the hospital. Can't say I blame them to some extent. I mean, you go to school to help preserve life, and you end up preserving death. Kind of a weird turn of events, if you ask me.

So where do I fit into all this?

Picture yourself with a loved one who's died and come back to life. They don't seem to recognize who you are and, now and then, they might try to eat you. You're not allowed to shoot them, because it's illegal. *Any* form of cruelty toward zombies now is considered a hate crime, believe it or not.

You do your best for them, after all this could be a parent, child, spouse, etc. You even put them in one of these homes or asylums, hoping they'll get the care they need.

Then, you realize they're not being cared for at all. They're simply set free during the day to roam around the grounds aimlessly, and fed raw meat four or five times a day. Then tied down at night—since zombies don't sleep—while staff watch movies or sleep.

This whole set-up was put in place to preserve the quality of life. The problem is, how is this doing that? There is no quality of life.

We're talking about people who can understand what is going on around them. They hear us speaking to them and understand what we say. They have thoughts and are probably trying to communicate those thoughts to us, but aren't able to. They can only move at a rate of about two feet per minute and have no speech capabilities. Not to mention the decomposition of the body. People are watching their loved ones waste away.

This doesn't sound like much of a life to me. Most people who have someone in their life who's been turned into a zombie tend to agree with me, and these people become my clients.

I like to think most of them come to me because I realize zombies are still people and still have cognitive thought, and I treat them as such, while others in the same line of work act just like those cops on zombie duty. They go around killing zombies as if they were twelve-year-olds playing the latest video game.

That isn't how I roll, so to speak.

The asylum was like a fortress. Fortunately, I had an easy way in.

The first few times I had come here when I first opened up shop, I entered under the guise of being a visitor. I'm smart enough to realize this ruse wouldn't work for very long. It doesn't take a genius to notice a dead zombie every time I'm there, and they'd eventually pick up on the fact that I'm visiting a different one every time I go there. I needed to figure something else out.

One good thing about once having been a cop, you learn a few tricks on how to commit crimes. I was able to swipe a set of keys during one of my pretend visits and the nice thing about many hospitals—mental hospitals specifically—is there are so many doors always locked up, so they tend to use one key for the majority of them. Sunny Vale Mental Health Center was no exception. I only needed to make a copy of one key to get in where I needed to be.

It's very nice of the good nurses at the asylum to make my job easier.

The other thing was, there was only one security guard on at night. Most of you reading this are probably thinking what I thought the first time I found this out: it's never a good idea to only have one guard on at any given time, mostly as a safety precaution. Having said that, the reality of the situation is security companies are in business to make money. They don't care about their guards and prove this by saving money on wages by paying them very little money and having as few as possible on duty at any given time.

Due to this, I was able to walk through the front door and walk past the security office where the underpaid and overly disgruntled guard sat at his desk watching a movie on his laptop, and who didn't even bother to glance up at me since he must have assumed I was a staff member coming in late or who had gone for a coffee run. Either way, I had made it past my first obstacle.

The second obstacle was no greater challenge. The door to the switchboard office was always closed. All I had to do was duck under the window and sneak right past it to the stairwell.

I went to the top floor, up the back stairway which led to a fire exit. I knew this was the best way to go since the door was not connected to the alarm and I would not have to go anywhere near the nursing station. The door led into the hallway just outside the patients' rooms.

Every time I walked onto the ward, my heart sank. I don't consider myself to be the most sensitive person in the world, but I hated seeing people treated like animals. My first time on the ward, when I pretended to be a visitor, it was during the daytime. The zombies were allowed to wander around the floor, but the nurses kept themselves at their station, behind shatter-proof glass. They never left except to throw food out for the patients a few times a day.

At night, they were put in five-point restraints. This meant both wrists, both ankles, and their chests were tied down to restrict just about all movement. This allowed the night staff to feel safer, I suppose, but I still felt it was a violation of the zombies' rights.

Once I was through the door, I made my way to where the rooms were. I checked all the rooms until I found one with a bed marked EDWARDS, GLORIA. This must be Nathan's mother.

I walked to the side of the bed and knelt on one knee, looking at the shell in front of me.

"Gloria," I whispered. She turned her head to face me, recognizing her name. "My name is Tom. I'm a friend of Nathan's." I could have sworn she tried to smile when I said her son's name. Her eyes *did* light up.

I waited a moment for her to register what I had said—there's not telling how fast a zombie's brain processes information—before continuing. "He asked me to come here to help you. He told me you're suffering."

This is the part that separates me from the other "hitmen" who do this. For me to do this right, without any violation of a person's freewill, I need their permission before doing anything. This is why I made sure Nathan understood my method of operation. There are no guarantees in the way I do things. However, if the patient turns down my offer, the client is refunded any money paid in advance. I only charge if the service is performed. I'm an honest businessman.

"Do you feel you're suffering, Gloria?"

I waited for a full minute before she nodded slowly.

"Would you like me to end your suffering?"

It took almost two minutes this time, but she nodded again.

"You realize this means I will end your life?" Okay, "life" may be a poor choice of word in this case, but there's no other way to say it. Either way, she nodded a third time, which meant I was able to move on to the procedure.

I reached into my pocket and removed a syringe I had prepared before leaving the office. This made things a lot quicker. The syringe contained an anesthetic that would dull any pain. I had promised Nathan—as I did all my clients—I would do this humanely. Which meant, the patient would feel as little pain as possible.

Before I could do anything, I heard faint footsteps coming down the hall toward me. I quickly and quietly got down on my stomach and pulled myself under Gloria's bed in time to see a pair of white shoes with legs sticking out of them enter the room. They walked right up to Gloria's bed, only a foot away from my face.

Did they know I was there?

I held my breath, terrified of being caught. Since killing zombies had been turned into a hate crime, the punishment was severe.

The nurse seemed to be checking something, though from my position under the bed I couldn't tell what, then walked over to each bed and seemed to do the same thing before leaving the room.

I let out my breath but waited a few minutes to make sure the nurse wasn't coming back.

Once back on my feet, I rolled Gloria over onto her side, stuck the needle into her spinal cord, and pressed on the plunger until the fluid inside had emptied. Then I let her roll onto her back once again and waited a few more moments for the medication to take effect. I wanted to make sure this was done right.

One thing about this job is when trying to be silent, it's difficult to find good ways to kill someone when you have to disable the brain.

A gunshot to the head works wonders, but it's way too loud.

I found the best way was with a hammer and spike. A couple of quick taps and it was all over.

I used one of those small hammers that came in the pocket-sized toolkits, for portability. The spike was about six inches long. I made sure to wear gloves too. You can never be too careful.

I placed the spike in the middle of her forehead and held the hammer just above it. I could almost swear there was a tear rolling down her cheek.

"Nathan wanted me to tell you he loves you. He asked me to do this because he can't bear to see you suffer anymore, Gloria. He only wants what's best for you."

Then the hammer came down. Once. Twice. After a third time, the job was done. I didn't bother to remove the nail when it was over. I just got the hell out of there as fast as I could without making any noise.

When I got back to my car, I let myself cry. It never got any easier. Even though I'd done this dozens of times, I still felt like a cold-hearted killer.

I drove to my apartment in complete silence. I had no wish to listen to the radio. I just wanted to be alone with my thoughts for the moment.

Since my wife left me and got the house, I decided an apartment was all I needed. I even thought of getting rid of that and living in my office, but I needed a home away from work. Somewhere I could go and not be disturbed.

There were no messages on my answering machine when I got home, which was a relief. I was thinking of taking some time off. I needed some time to heal emotionally and mentally. I think the job was getting to me. I'd quit, but this business needs someone who does things right. Someone who does it because he cares about people.

I figured I must be doing something right. I mean, even my ex's husband had come to see me when she and my daughter turned. He said he knew I would do it so they wouldn't suffer.

He was wrong.

Dead wrong.

I walked into the room and turned on the light so I could see the two figures tied up, leaning against the wall.

I walked over to them.

"Hi, honey," I said, kissing Dianne on the cheek.

"Good night, princess." I gave Laura a peck as well.

Maybe one day I'll be able to build up enough courage to bring myself to end their suffering. But so far, I haven't been able to bring myself to do it.

FEAR ITSELF

"I appreciate you helping me out with my thesis."

Jeremy said nothing. He just stared at Mike, eyes moving side to side, following him as he paced back and forth

"All those other people who tried to help were useless," Mike continued. "All I wanted to do was an in-depth study of fear. Find out what scares people. I wanted to get right down to the root of the problem. Learn what triggered their fear and how it developed over the years. My goal was to figure out what it feels like to be exposed to something that truly terrifies you."

Mike stopped pacing for a brief moment. Just long enough to glance over at Jeremy to make sure he was still paying attention. "You know what those other people gave me? Squat. I asked them what scares them and they gave answers like harm coming to loved ones, poverty, sickness, and death. Not a single one of them had an original answer. Well, there was that one guy who had jangelaphobia. Know what that is? It's a fear of gelatinous substances...like Jell-O

He chuckled at the memory. "I know," he contin-ued. "It's not nice to laugh at other people's phobias. Especially for someone who's studying to become a psychiatrist, like myself. But come on. Fear of Jell-O? I thought the guy was joking at first, so I asked him to come back the next day. I brought a bowl of Jell-O with me to see what would happen." Mike started laughing even harder now. "He wouldn't come out from under the table until I took it out of the room. Man, that guy needed serious help. How can I use this guy as a case study for a thesis? Who'd believe me? My professor would think I made the whole thing up."

Mike paused for a moment.

"Would you stop looking at me like that? Yes, I am aware of how unprofessional it is for me to laugh at this guy, but I can't help it. Besides, this whole psychi-atry thing wasn't even my idea. It was my mother's. She thought I'd be good at it because apparently, I'm sensitive and understanding of others. Go figure. Have I got her fooled or what?"

Another laugh.

"But seriously, I'm only doing this because she had such high hopes for me and I don't want to let her down like my brother. He went downhill and got into drugs, the whole bit. We lost contact with him over a year ago and we don't even know if he's dead or in jail. Once he started heading down the wrong path, I de-cided that I would have to be the one to step up and make Mom proud. That's why I was so disappointed with those other people I interviewed. I knew I could never write a good thesis using those idiots as case studies.

For a while there, I thought I let Mom down."

He stopped short and turned to face Jeremy. "And then, out of nowhere, it hit me. The solution to my problem. What I needed to do was to track a fear right from the moment of its conception and study it as it continues to grow into a full-blown phobia. Sounds hard, doesn't it? I mean, I'd have to be there at the exact moment that someone becomes afraid of something. What are the odds of that? The only way I could be sure it happened was to trigger the fear myself."

Mike walked around Jeremy and placed a hand on his shoulder. "And that's where you come in, my friend." He noticed that Jeremy was shaking, and was pleased by that fact. "Had I asked you yesterday when we first met what you were afraid of, what would you have said?" He waited a moment as if expecting the other man to answer then continued. "Would you have given me one of those stock answers like all the others? Probably not. You're young, in good shape. You still think you're invincible. You probably would have told me you weren't afraid of anything."

Mike walked over to the table a few feet away and began to examine the instruments. He would save the good ones for later. The knife would suffice for their first session. Then he walked back over to Jeremy. Once the young man saw the knife in Mike's hand, he began to whimper, and tears started down his cheeks.

"See how perfect this is? You weren't afraid of me yesterday. But I'm sure you are now. And as the weeks go by, I'll get to watch that fear become more intense. This is going to be a great thesis." He began to cut into Jeremy's arm. He could see his captive's eyes grow even wider as he struggled to free himself from his bonds. At the same time, he was yelling something, but Mike wasn't able to distinguish what that something might be through the gag.

"Oh yes, this is going to be fun," Mike said, ignoring Jeremy's screams. "Mom is going to be so proud."

YESTERDAY'S SINS

Ryan's hands were shaking as he reached to open the door leading into Shelley's Diner. He had no idea why he was so nervous, but there was a weird feeling in the pit of his stomach as he pulled the door open. He'd only had that same feeling once before, his wedding day.

As he yanked the door open, the aroma of hamburgers and fries wafted out. For a moment, the pleasant scent of cooked food made him forget his original purpose in coming, but then it all came flooding back.

He stood there a few moments, holding the door wide open as if letting someone else go in before him, but no one was there. When he realized what he was doing, he felt foolish and hoped no one had noticed.

Having never been to Shelley's before, Ryan had no idea how busy it would be. It was crowded, the din of customers making it hard to listen. Add that to the sound of food cooking on a grill from the kitchen, dishes clattering as busboys cleaned empty tables, and a bell notifying the waitresses that orders were up. Ryan never did like crowds, so his first instinct was to turn around and leave, but curiosity got the better of him. He needed to find out why he had been summoned.

Despite the racket and the large number of patrons, Ryan was able to find Jerry with no trouble. He was, after all, a huge man. His beer gut had gotten even bigger since the last time Ryan had seen him and his bushy beard showed traces of grey that hadn't been there before. He had wild, unpredictable eyes, making him appear either slightly child-like or insane.

Just as he was walking over to the table, Jerry looked up and grinned in recognition. He stood up to shake Ryan's hand.

"So good to see you, my friend," Jerry said in his deep, booming voice. His excitement didn't seem quite genuine.

"Yeah, it's been awhile."

"Almost fifteen years, I think."

"That long, eh?" Even as he spoke, Ryan's eyes were glued to the white-collar that contrasted with an all-black outfit. At first, he was taken aback, thinking that his friend had only called him after all these years to try and save his soul.

Jerry chuckled. "I see you noticed the collar."

"Yeah. Can't say I'm too surprised, though. I mean, you were always the more religious one of the group."

"I prefer the term spiritual." He motioned to an empty chair. "Are you hungry?"

Ryan shook his head as he sat in the chair. "I thought priests weren't supposed to drink," he said, noticing a half-full bottle of Budweiser and two empties on the table.

The priest shrugged. "I don't see the harm in having a beer now and then. Want one?"

Ryan shook his head and when the waitress came by to take his order, he asked for coffee. Once she left, Ryan turned his attention back to his old friend.

"So, what made you get in touch with me after all these years?"

"Cutting right to the chase, are we?" Jerry chuckled again, leaning in closer and lowering his voice. "I figured you should be the first to hear this since you were the only one I told I was going to do it."

"Do what?"

The priest had a smug look on his face. "Remember when we were kids and I told you something I always wanted to do?"

"Get laid?"

Jerry burst out with a laugh that seemed a bit much for such a poor joke. Ryan got the impression that he was merely being polite.

"No, the other thing. Come on, you have to remember. It's something I promised I would do someday, no matter how long it took."

He searched his memory and managed to come up with a conversation the two of them had when they were younger, not even teenagers yet. He couldn't remember the entire conversation, but he knew it had something to do with angels.

"You don't mean..." Ryan trailed off. He couldn't even voice the idea. It was too absurd.

Jerry nodded. "Yep. I did it."

"You couldn't have. It's not even possible."

"It's possible. It took me ten years, but I finally found a way to do it."

"How?"

"I'll let you in on that little secret later on."

"Can I see it?"

The smug grin came back. "I was hoping you'd ask."

Both men quickly finished their drinks then left the restaurant.

———

Jerry's home looked like an apartment without a building attached to it. It looked tiny. The church seemed almost just as small. From the outside, it looked like it might be able to fit a congregation of fifty people.

If that.

Ryan, not being religious, had no idea how the hierarchy of the priesthood worked. He never knew how one priest got the huge cathedrals with hundreds of parishioners, while others were stuck with these dinky little buildings not much bigger than a Vegas wedding chapel.

"Well, here we are," Jerry announced. "Welcome to my humble abode."

Ryan felt like saying, "You got the humble part right," but decided to keep the opinion to himself.

When they walked in, the house looked smaller on the inside than on the outside. The furniture made it look cramped and Ryan had to maneuver around a bit to make his way through the living room.

"So, where is it?"

The large man let out another chuckle. "Impatient, aren't we?" He waited for a moment as if expecting Ryan to answer. "Don't worry. It's downstairs."

As they walked, Ryan asked him, "Are you going to tell me how you caught it?"

"All in due time, my friend. All in due time."

Jerry opened a door in the kitchen that led to a set of stairs leading down into an unfinished basement.

"Unfortunately, the house is paid for by the diocese. They don't like to shell out for luxuries like comfort," Jerry explained. "Well, not when you're the priest of a very small parish." There was no laugh this time, so Ryan couldn't tell if he was being good-natured or if the statement was one of bitterness.

When he reached the bottom of the stairs, nothing could have prepared Ryan for what he was about to see. He hadn't thought that Jerry was serious. Being good-natured, Jerry also tended to play practical jokes. Now that he was in the basement, he realized his friend hadn't been joking at all.

The beast chained to the concrete wall had long, thin legs with feet that had three talon-like claws. Its torso, while still skinny, also looked like it had some muscle tone. There were more claws on its hands that looked as though they could tear a person in half with only one swipe. Its face was almost oblong, and two long teeth protruded from its mouth. They looked sharper than its claws. Its entire body was a dull gray color, except for the bat-like wings which were more of a charcoal.

"Beautiful, isn't it?" Jerry remarked as he gazed up at the figure before them.

"Beautiful? Are you kidding me? This thing looks like it belongs in a horror movie."

"What did you expect? A halo and harp?"

"Well...yeah."

"Well, the Bible never does give an accurate description of what angels look like."

"Yeah, but still..." Ryan took a step toward it and as he did so the creature let out a loud screech, almost deafening him. When he looked over, he noticed the priest was covering his ears.

"What the hell was that?" Ryan asked once the sound had finally faded.

Jerry smiled. "If you liked that, you should hear it sing."

"It sings?"

"Beautifully. It's so magical; it almost puts me into a trance when I hear it."

"Does it do anything else?"

"Well, there is one thing..." Jerry trailed off and Ryan got the impression he was afraid of something. Regaining his composure, the priest continued, "But I'd rather you saw it for yourself."

Ryan was about to press the matter, then decided against it. Instead, he asked, "How did you catch it?"

"The story of Elisha."

"Who the hell is Elisha?"

"A biblical prophet. There's a story when he and his servant were attacked by the Syrian army. The servant thought it was the two of them against the whole army, but Elisha prayed for God to reveal his angels, and hundreds of them appeared before the young man."

"I don't get it."

"The angels were invisible until Elisha prayed for them to be revealed to his servant. I also know everyone has a guardian angel that is with us at all times, protecting us. So, I prayed for mine to be revealed and there it was."

"And you caught it."

"It was quite a struggle, but I managed."

"So, now what?"

"What do you mean?"

"Well, you've caught this thing. Now what? Put it on display? Use it to become rich and famous?"

"I'm insulted you'd even imply that I would do something like that."

"Then what's the point of all this?"

"Proof," Jerry told him. He still kept his eyes on the angel, as if even he couldn't believe he had caught this magnificent being. "Once I reveal this angel to the world, no one would be able to deny the existence of God. Everyone would have to believe. With this one creature, I can save the world."

Ryan felt the priest was deluding himself but didn't want to stomp on his dream, or his "life's work" as Jerry had called it. "Wow. This is way too much for me to handle in one night."

"You're right. It's getting late. We should go to bed. Why don't you stay the night?"

"Oh, I don't want to impose."

What Ryan meant was he didn't think the house was big enough for two people, but he didn't want to offend Jerry.

"Oh, it's no imposition. I can take the couch, and you can have my room."

"Well, I'll stay, but I'll take the couch."

Jerry smiled once again. "Suit yourself."

While he slept, Ryan dreamed. Except, they weren't dreams so much as memories. The scene had happened almost ten years ago and he had almost forgotten it. He had tried so hard to forget it. But now, the small details came rushing back to him and he knew that everything he saw now was exactly as it happened.

Ryan found himself watching the scene, not from his own point of view, but that of an onlooker viewing the scene as if perched in the branch of a tree and could see a younger version of himself.

He saw this younger self crouched behind a shrub, watching Brad Denton as he worked. Ryan remembered how he had checked into the man, found out he worked for a landscaping company. After that, it was easy to figure out exactly where he was working.

Since all the other workers were at the front of the house, he felt sure no one would hear anything, since they were at the rear and far enough into the bush.

So all he had to do now was wait.

As he watched the scene unfold before him, he had to wonder what he'd been thinking. He looked at Brad, no shirt, hauling around armfuls of branches, carrying small logs over his shoulder. There didn't seem to be an ounce of fat anywhere on the man's body.

Then, he looked at himself. Years of abusing his body with tobacco, caffeine, alcohol, and junk food had already begun to take their toll. Ryan was disgusted at how he aged before his time. His hair was thinning and he had a spare tire that he kept promising himself to do something about, but never got around to doing anything.

Since he hadn't had the foresight to bring even so much as a pocket knife for a weapon, he was outmatched. It almost made him cringe to realize how dumb he'd been.

It was that moment when the younger Ryan realized this and turned to make his way back to his car, still crouching to remain unseen. He didn't make it very far when his foot kicked something hard.

The older Ryan didn't have to wait to find out what it was he had kicked. He remembered exactly what it was.

A chainsaw.

Even now he wondered what would have happened if he had never bothered to pick it up. How would things be different if he had taken a slightly different route and had never happened upon it?

His hands shook as he reached down to pick up the saw. It was a smaller one, very light weight. Shaking it, he could hear the swishing of gasoline inside.

He made his way back to his original position behind the shrub and waited for his opportunity. As it turned out, luck was on his side again, as Brad appeared to be working late that day, most likely due to being behind in his work and wanting to catch up.

Dusk was settling when Brad had finally decided to quit for the day and walked toward the house. The shrub Ryan used as cover was directly off a trail, so he figured the target would most likely walk right past him on his way.

He'd been right. The younger man was walking toward him, his T-shirt slung over his shoulder and still wearing his work gloves.

The older Ryan wanted to yell at him, to warn him, but he discovered, as he already suspected, he had no control over the outcome. Things would play out exactly as they had before.

All he could do was watch himself lunge at Brad and yank on the ripcord at the same time. The roar of the tiny chainsaw was almost deafening. The motor itself wasn't loud. Ryan suspected it was simply his imagination increasing the volume.

As he watched this, bits of another scene played through his mind. Sporadic images of Brad with Ryan's wife, Sandra, flashed before his eyes. He had walked in on them one day, and for a long time afterward was unable to get the image of Brad's face as he mounted the adulteress from behind out of his head.

Even though he had walked out of the room and never returned, never saw or spoke to his wife again, he harbored a hatred toward Brad unlike any he'd ever felt before. A hatred that had driven him to kill another human being.

Sandra's lover was taken by surprise and had no time to react. By the time he realized what was happening, the saw was already digging its way through his skull.

He kept the chainsaw embedded in Brad's head until the man fell to his knees. At that point, Ryan figured the only thing keeping Brad from falling over was the fact that he was holding him up with the chainsaw. He struggled to yank it out, using all his strength. Finally, he was able to jerk the saw free.

Once the chainsaw was removed, the body fell face-first to the ground, convulsed for a moment or two, then remained perfectly still.

The first part of his plan was complete, burying the body where it lay was the only thing left for him to do.

Since the job had not been completed, he figured the workers would have left their tools behind so they were ready to begin work immediately the next day. He found a shovel leaning up against the house, and he returned to where he had left the body and began to dig.

He woke from his dream, wondering what could have caused the memories to have come back to him so vividly after trying to ignore them for so long.

He got up from the couch and wandered into the kitchen to get a drink of water. The clock on the stove told him it was 3 am, and he could hear snoring coming from one of the rooms down the hall. Ryan assumed it was Jerry.

Another sound grabbed his attention. It was coming from below him. It sounded like singing.

Ryan walked about halfway down the steps and listened. From somewhere in the basement, came the most beautiful music he'd ever heard. An immediate calm came over him as he continued to get closer and listened to the entrancing sound.

The singing stopped before he reached the bottom of the steps. Since there was no one else in the basement, he figured it must have been the angel.

"You should hear it sing," Jerry had said.

He approached the creature who was now staring at Ryan, following his every move.

"I liked your singing."

The angel did not respond.

"Could you sing some more for me?"

Again, it showed no sign of understanding.

Both creature and man regarded each other for a long time. Ryan, beginning to feel awkward, finally broke the silence.

"I had a dream, you know." He paced the room as

he spoke, the angel following him with its eyes. "I have a feeling it had something to do with you. I mean, it had to. I haven't thought about that day in a long time. This can't be a coincidence."

He stopped pacing long enough to turn and face the creature for a moment. "What do you want from me?"

When it didn't respond, he continued walking.

Ryan let out a chuckle. "You know, this almost reminds me of one of those cheesy movies of the week. This would be the part where I realize what I did was wrong and repent and everything's okay." He walked past a workbench and let his fingers run across the various tools laid out on the surface. When they touched a hatchet, he stopped to pick it up in his hands.

"Here's the problem," he said. "You can't exist."

The angel gave him a puzzled look, which was the first time it showed any sign it understood what he was saying.

"I spent my whole life believing there was nothing out there. Especially after I killed Brad. I mean, if there's no God, then I don't have to worry about it, right? But now," he walked toward the angel, hatchet in hand, "things have changed."

He stopped within a few feet of the creature. "I came so close to forgetting about Brad's death. Almost as if it never happened. It took me a long time to get rid of the guilt, and then you come along and bring it all back in the space of a few hours."

There was a short pause as he gazed at the beast one more time, noticing the puzzled look had been replaced by one of fear as if it was reading his mind.

"But if you're dead," Ryan continued, "then you

can't make me remember anymore." He raised the weapon above his head. "Please, don't take this personally. I just can't take the memories anymore. This is the only way I can move on."

He lunged, burying the hatchet in the angel's head. A thick, white substance, almost slimy, squirted out, covering Ryan as the angel fell to the ground.

Leaving the ax buried in the creature's skull, he turned to make his way back to the staircase, noticing an odor in the air that hadn't been there before. Sulfur? Brimstone? He couldn't be sure, but it was forgotten completely once a feeling of panic overwhelmed him. He knew he couldn't stay in this house. What would Jerry say when he found out Ryan had killed the angel?

But he didn't move. He stood there, staring down at the creature, instantly regretting what he'd done. He felt a tightness, almost squeezing sensation, in his chest making it difficult for him to breathe. His heart seemed to beat faster now. He attributed this to remorse.

He was distracted from these symptoms as the singing started once again, this time sounding as if choked by tears. Ryan hadn't taken his eyes off the creature, who still lay on the floor, unmoving.

He turned and saw another angel climbing the stairs. Where had that one come from? he wondered. He didn't have an answer, but it was obvious it was the second angel who sang as it wept, its voice fading as it climbed the steps and left the basement.

Something wrenched in Ryan's chest. The tightness he'd felt moments before had slowly expanded into pain, which seemed to be moving into his neck and shoulders.

He doubled over, holding his chest as the pain increased, eventually bringing him to his knees. He tried to call out, hoping Jerry would hear him, but he found he couldn't utter a sound as he fell to the floor completely, next to the lifeless body of the angel.

Jerry's words echoed in his mind about guardian angels. The priest had told him everyone had one. Jerry had also mentioned the one he'd caught was his own. Ryan briefly wondered what it meant for his friend now that he'd murdered it. Had he doomed the priest? He couldn't know for sure.

He forgot about it once he realized the one he saw leaving moments ago must have been...Oh no, Ryan thought as the realization took hold. No, it's not possible.

He didn't have time to let this new knowledge sink in, as he found himself slowly fading.

He opened his eyes and saw he was no longer in Jerry's basement. Instead, he was in a room, which he instantly recognized as once being his bedroom. But that was a long time ago, back when he and Sandra had still been together.

At first, he thought it might be another memory, but realized it was different. He wasn't viewing the scene from outside himself as before. He was in the room.

He didn't understand how he came to be in the house he once lived in. Since he hadn't spoken to Sandra in almost ten years, he couldn't be sure if even she still resided there.

He was interrupted by noises. He turned his head and saw Brad and Sandra on the bed, which confused him since he knew Brad had been dead for close to ten years.

Slowly, the familiarity of the scene dawned on him. This was exactly how it looked ten years ago when it had inadvertently walked in on them. The stench of sweat. Sandra on her knees, her face buried in the mattress. Brad, behind her, too intent on his thrusting to notice anyone else in the room. The look of intense pleasure on Brad's face made Ryan want to vomit.

Ryan could stand no more of this. He lunged for the door and pulled as hard as he could, only to find it locked. He kept pulling, though he knew it was useless, even putting his foot up on the wall to brace himself. The door wouldn't budge.

He banged on it as loud as he could, screaming until his throat hurt. No one came. And obviously, the lovers couldn't hear him since the noise he made didn't seem to phase them one bit.

Finally, exhausted, he turned and slunk down to the floor, back against the wall. He put his head in his hands, sobbing, as he realized what was happening.

He was trapped in this memory.

Something inside him—morbid curiosity, most likely—made him look up at the two lovers. He couldn't take his eyes off them, even though it caused him such emotional torment to watch, and the thought occurred to him that this was his eternal punishment. His personal version of hell.

It might have been Ryan's imagination, but for a split second, he could have sworn Brad winked at him.

ANCESTORS

IF NOT FOR THE TORCH TO LIGHT THE WAY, NONE OF them would have been able to see even a foot in front of them. It was night and the trees blocked out the moon, so no light spilled into the cave. The flame lit enough of the area in front of them so they could muddle their way through. Many were beginning to think they were wasting there as the only sound the splashing of their feet through the shallow water was the only sound any of them could hear.

Without a clue as to whether they even had the right cave, they went on, each man's face showing resolve, each one determined to not return home until their task had been carried out. None seemed to even consider their deaths an option, though somewhere in the back of their minds, the possibility existed.

None of them spoke. There was no need. Each of them knew what they were there to do. Though they hadn't sat down and worked out a plan of action, their goal had been made clear.

Most of them held rifles—or at least pistols—but there were some who, due to an aversion to guns or a lack of financial means to obtain one, opted for large sticks fashioned into spears. Either way, all twenty-three men were armed.

Now and then, Jarrod, their self-proclaimed leader, would stop and hold up his hand, signaling the others to do likewise. He would listen for a few moments then continue on.

Michael wondered about Jarrod. Mostly he wondered about the man's motives. The hunt had been his idea in the first place and Michael couldn't help but wonder if it was even necessary. After all, was the risk worth it for a few animals?

He'd tried to bring this up before, but Jarrod had riled up the mob to the point where logic was no longer a part of the equation. They set off on their mission immediately, taking only enough time to grab their weapons. Michael assumed this was to prevent anyone from being able to take the time to think the whole thing through and allow common sense to prevail. So when he protested, Michael was seen as a coward and traitor to the village, forced to participate to avoid being lynched.

At least this way he had a chance for survival, even if it was a small one.

Which was why he found himself trudging through the cave, albeit grudgingly. The men had never used their guns for anything other than scaring crows or killing food and now thought they were capable of using those same weapons to kill a monster. Michael was aware none of them were fighters any more than they were knights in shining armor on their way to slay a dragon and rescue the princess. Though that's how they seemed to view themselves. Michael, however, saw things as they were. They were a pack of squirrels on their way to pick a fight with a grizzly bear over a few stolen nuts.

Jarrod stopped yet again, holding his hand up as always, silencing the sound of the men wading through the water. He stood there longer than usual. His one hand holding the torch, the other still up to indicate no one move, talk, or even breathe.

Michael guessed the others wondered the same thing as he: what exactly was he listening for?

"Hear anything?" came a voice from the back of the group, shouting loud enough for Jarrod to hear him. Though Michael couldn't see the speaker, the voice sounded like that of Thomas Riley.

Jarrod took just enough time to turn around and shush him before turning his attention back to the front.

"Well, geez," the speaker continued, "we've been walking through this cave for what seems like forever and we haven't found a single thing. Maybe we should try a different cave."

"Will you shut up?" Jarrod's impatience was visible in the glow of the torch. "We don't want the beast to know we're coming."

"Oh yeah. `Cuz we've been ever so quiet so far. It's not like we sound like a herd of elephants stomping through the water the way we have. If there's a monster in this cave he's probably died of laughter at how stupid we are by now."

Jarrod ignored him. "We're getting close."

It was Michael's turn to pipe in. "How could you possibly know that?"

The group's leader exaggeratedly sniffed the air. "Smell that?"

"Yeah." Riley again. "Smells like your feet."

"No, seriously. Don't you smell that?"

The odor was so faint, Michael hadn't noticed it until it was pointed out to him. Though, now that he had, he knew exactly what Jarrod was thinking. Each time the monster attacked, there was a lingering stench that always remained for hours afterward. The same stench hanging in the almost indescribable air, though Michael would have compared it to the combination of rotting flesh, sweat, and feces. He held his breath in an attempt to keep from gagging. Many of the others were now lifting their shirts over their noses trying to keep the stench at bay.

"Come on. It can't be too much further. We have to keep going."

It was obvious to Michael some of the men were beginning to second guess their spontaneous decision. It seemed this was all now becoming a bit too real. Maybe they hadn't truly believed there was any such creature, but now the realization was dawning on them that there was and fear was setting in.

But Jarrod walked on and the rest followed, much to Michael's dismay as he was hoping the group would be deterred.

They rounded the next corner only to find Jarrod had stopped again. This time, though, he didn't hold up his hand as he seemed to be paralyzed. At first, Michael wondered what was going, but as he looked at the light given off by the torch, he caught a glimpse of the same thing Jarrod had. The spiked tip of a tail.

Once the others noticed, they let out a gasp, almost as one. All of them stood in place. The moment they'd been anticipating and not a single one of them acted.

Jarrod slowly moved the torch to the left, revealing more of the creature's spiked, reptilian body. As he watched in awe, Michael thought this may be a dinosaur who had managed to survive undetected all these years much like others who only existed in legend, like the Loch Ness monster.

As the light moved closer to the creature's head, Michael silently prayed the creature had not woken, but when it was fully revealed, its visible eye was open, staring right at them.

He was too entranced by the enormous beast in front of them to even utter a sound. All the men could have stood in a line and most likely would not equal its length. Its mouth was huge and Michael was certain it could have swallowed any one of them whole whenever it chose to do so.

He flinched when he saw the mouth move, fully expecting it to devour one of them to demonstrate what they were up against.

"So, you've finally come," the creature said, its voice sounded wet as if it were slurping a drink as it talked, forcing Michael to strain to understand what it said.

For the first few moments, its words were met with shocked silence until finally, Jarrod answered. "You can speak?"

"The fact that I can speak is not important. But what I have to say is."

"Nothing you have to say can deter us from what we have come here to do." Even Michael could hear the trembling in their leader's voice and was sure the creature had no fear of any of them.

The beast let out a sigh. "I have no intention of deterring you. Only to warn you." It paused and glanced around as if to make sure everyone present was paying attention to it. "You shouldn't have come here. You are all doomed."

Jarrod let out an unconvincing laugh. "You're outnumbered, beast. I think you are the one who is doomed."

"You misunderstand the situation." The creature shifted one of its hind feet and that's when Michael noticed the length of the talon-like claws had to be at least as long as the shotgun he held, if not longer.

"Perhaps you'd care to enlighten us?" Michael knew Jarrod was trying to sound patronizing to intimidate the beast, but his voice was still shaky and couldn't have fooled a child.

"I was once like you," the creature told them. "I was once a man."

This time, Jarrod's laugh seemed genuine. "You? A man? I don't believe you."

"Believe what you want, but I know the truth. All I ask is that you hear me out before you kill me."

Michael glanced around at his companions. All of them still held their weapons but none had taken aim. Either they were paralyzed by fright or just curious as to what it had to say.

Jarrod must have noticed the same thing, as he turned to the creature and said, "Alright. We're listening."

"As I said, I was once a man. I lived in the same village you call home. Also like you, the village was tormented by monsters who killed our livestock at night, threatening our livelihood. In those days, my name was Edward Talbot."

Michael was shocked into awareness. This creature had the same last name as himself. How could this be? he thought. Everyone else had caught on to the connection as during the dramatic pause, all eyes were on him until the beast's voice once again cut through the silence.

"To ensure our village could survive, we decided we had to track down these monsters and destroy every last one of them. The decision was unanimous among the villagers. Well, the men anyway. Our wives thought we were foolish to risk our lives over a few cows, as they put it. But to us, our honor was at stake. We couldn't let these beings, whatever they were, take away our livelihood or drive us away from our homes.

"As far as we could see, fighting was the only solution available to us.

"We had picked a night where the moon shined bright enough to light our way, but this did us no good as we discovered the monsters lived in caves. None of us owned guns, so we had brought whatever sharp objects we could.

"Of course, none of us had ever seen them so we had no idea how truly immense they were. Had we known, we may not have ventured out.

"There were only sixteen men in the village able to go. All males under eighteen stayed behind in case we didn't return. It would do no good to have all the men die. Of course, those who were too old also stayed behind as they would have been useless against such creatures.

"We were farmers, not trackers. We wandered through the woods aimlessly, hoping to stumble upon some sign of these creatures we hunted. We knew nothing about them other than they killed our animals. They could be hiding anywhere and we knew we would only find them by pure chance.

"I can't recall who, but one of our group had

somehow strayed and stumbled upon a cave none of us had known even existed. Of course, we never had any reason to venture out into the woods, so there was no way we could have known about it.

"We almost disregarded it as from the outside, the cave didn't look very deep and we thought it a poor place to hide. But on further inspection, we noticed it went deep into the ground. So we gathered the men and went inside.

"We were amazed at just how deep it went. It didn't take long for us to realize there was no way it was natural. Someone—or something—had to have dug it. And for something of that magnitude, whatever it was had to have been something big.

"Thought our fear grew, we pressed onward. I'm not sure it was about the survival of those who lived in the village as much as the embarrassment of returning home to our wives and children and having to admit we failed. Most of us would have rather died than admit cowardice. So we pressed onward.

"I won't bore you with the details of making our way through the cave. We were all relieved that it was a straight path and didn't fork. By the time we had found it, we were too tired and impatient to have to deal with trying to get to the end of a maze.

"It took a long time, but we finally made our way to the end and found ourselves face to face with one of the beasts."

"The monster stared at us for a long time. A few of us had our weapons pointed at it, but most were too terrified to even move. As for me, I wondered why it had not attacked us yet. Surely a beast that size could have killed us all before we had a chance to react. Its massive tail alone could have wiped out half of us in one swoop.

"But the beast remained perfectly still.

"I was transfixed by its eyes, for I saw something in them I never thought I would see in the eyes of a monster. Thought at the time, I couldn't quite discern the emotion the eyes portrayed, I know now it was a combination of pain and pleading. Perhaps I was too frightened or too naïve, but after having too much time to look upon that day and replay every second of it in my mind, I can say beyond a shadow of a doubt, that creature was begging us to kill it. That's why it was lying there doing nothing to defend itself.

"I still find it strange how, when we set out from our homes, we were so determined to end this creature's life. But now that we were face to face with it, all of us were too scared to do anything. We gazed upon this thing with awe. I know I wondered more than once why God would create such a thing to dwell on the Earth. I saw no use for this being at all.

"Without any warning, the creature opened its massive jaws. I was certain it was going to attack us at that moment and I'm sure the others felt the same way because the suddenness drove all of us into action. Though, we did not have the opportunity to do much. As we ran toward the beast, our weapons aimed, someone from the back of the group had thrown his spear. We stopped and watched as it arced through the air, curious to see what would happen. Whoever it had been who'd thrown it, his aim was true. The spear struck the beast in the side of the head, spilling a greenish liquid I assumed to be its blood.

"The monster fell, but just before the spear had met its target, the creature had pierced the air with a loud noise. At first, I assumed the creature had cried out, having noticed the spear coming toward it. However, we had discussed it afterward and several of the men could have sworn it had yelled, `Wait!'

"I believe that to be the case, as I know now when the creature had opened its mouth, it was not trying to attack us. It was trying to speak. I firmly believe it was trying to give us the same warning that I am giving you now."

"And what warning might that be?" Jarrod asked, finally interrupting the beast's story. I know I—and I'm sure the rest of our group—wondered exactly what it was trying to tell us with its tale.

"There are fifteen other monsters in these woods, all hidden in caves. Once you have killed them all, please kill yourselves as well."

"That makes sixteen monsters in total," Jarrod observed. "The exact number of men in your party when you killed that monster. That's quite the coincidence."

"It's no coincidence. You see, that night all those years ago, we hunted every one of those monsters. Having killed that the first one gave us the courage we needed to find the rest and kill them. By the time we were satisfied that every one of them was dead, we were too tired to continue home, so we decided to sleep in the woods and return in the morning. But when we woke up, we realized we had been cursed. Our skin had become scaly and slimy. Just like a reptile. Just like one of those monsters. Those whose transformations were progressing faster than the rest had even begun to grow tails.

"We were becoming the very creatures we had just killed."

"Are you saying you have cursed us in this same

way?" Jarrod's voice was leery. Michael didn't think he believed a word of what the creature was saying.

"Maybe curse was the wrong word. Disease would be better. It's contagious. Simply by being near me, you have all been infected. Should you return to the village, you will infect the others and all those you love will be doomed. For their sakes, I ask you to wipe us out then kill yourselves. This is the only way to keep it from spreading."

The beast let out a sigh. "The ones we killed had been from the same village as us. This has been going on far too long."

"If you are from our village, how come we've never heard your name before?"

"How far back do your records go? I lived there three hundred years ago. This disease extends one's life, but it must be lived as a monster with urges to commit vile acts of murder. But we have regained some semblance of our humanity, which is why we only kill the animals and never the people of the village. You are, after all, our descendants."

Jarrod turned to face the mob. "Men! This creature is lying. Do not believe a word it says. It is trying to gain our sympathy so we'll spare its life and it will go on tormenting the village. We must kill it now."

Jarrod wasn't the only one who didn't believe the monster's words, as a shot rang out from the crowd and the beast fell immediately when the bullet struck it in the head. In a matter of seconds, its life had come to an end.

Just like in the story, the ease with which they had killed the first gave them the encouragement needed to go on and quickly dispel the rest. Just like the creature had said, they found fifteen others. This fact did not seem to be lost on any of them, which led to the discussion of what to do now the creatures had been dealt with.

"What if he spoke the truth?" more than one of them wondered aloud, but Jarrod kept brushing their worries aside, saying the beast was only trying to save its own life. Of course, none of them were buying his explanation, since it had practically begged them to wipe out its entire race.

"I don't think we can leave this up to chance," Michael offered, praying his words would be heeded this time around. "We're talking about our wives and children. Do we want to risk them becoming one of those things?"

They all nodded in unison. The lives of those left in the village and their descendants were at stake. No man wanted the weight of that responsibility on their shoulders.

So, it was decided they would do as the creature had asked, though no one seemed happy about it.

Those who had no guns were the first to go. The men who had brought firearms aimed, firing a single, close-range shot to the head, resulting in a quick and painless death. Several shots being fired at once made a loud, almost deafening explosion.

Michael knew this act would make killing himself that much easier, seeing as he knew he could no longer live with himself after taking the life of an innocent man. A quick look around him told him the others felt the same.

Each of the remaining villagers put their guns to their heads, each watching each other. Several of the men were in tears. Trembling. None of them had even considered the possibility the hunt would end in a mass suicide.

They counted: one, two three. Another deafening explosion as the men dropped, almost at the same moment. Blood pooled from their heads, forming one large puddle.

Jarrod lowered his pistol from his temple, took one last look at the bodies on the ground, and began to make his back to the village, scratching at a patch on his arm where a scale had already formed.

MONSTER

Patton yanked the door open only to find himself staring down the barrel of a handgun.

At first, he wanted to reach out and hug whoever was holding the weapon, thanking them profusely. But he managed to compose himself and stood there, showing no emotion.

With the gun staring him in the face, he was unable to focus on the person holding it, though he did have an inkling as to why.

"Are you Henry Patton?" The speaker's voice, which he also didn't recognize, sounded old and worn as if he had lived a lifetime of stress and heartache. The thick French accent didn't help Patton to place the intruder either.

Henry said nothing. He simply stood there knowing there was no action he could take quickly enough to avoid what was coming, so he waited for it to be over.

"I asked you a question."

"I heard you," Henry said. After living in the U.S. for almost fifty years, he had gotten so good at hiding his accent, he almost sounded like a genuine American. "But I figure if you've got a gun aimed at my head, you already know who I am. So, just get on with it."

He noticed the stranger hesitate for a moment. It was almost as if he was confused that Patton didn't show any fear.

"Look," Patton told him when he could no longer control his impatience. "If you're going to kill me, please get it over with. Otherwise, I'd like to get on with my day."

The other lowered the gun to his side, and for the first time, Patton was able to see his face. He was old—not as old as himself, but most likely in his sixties—and there was confusion on his face.

"My name is Jean Belanger."

Patton shook his head.

"My father was Michel Belanger."

"Should I recognize that name?"

"No, but I thought you would like to know the name of the man you killed. Well, one of them at least."

Patton had known from the moment he saw the gun that it had something to do with the war, but with everything that had occurred there, it was hard to pinpoint exactly what might have been the issue. However, seeing that this man was accusing him of murder and had a French name, the pieces were starting to come together.

He remembered that day clearly.

From his position at the fairground, he'd been able to smell smoke from buildings the soldiers chose to set on fire as they went from farm to farm, rounding up all of the people, which he thought was an odd thing to do since the villagers were told it was merely a routine check for weapons, and all innocent persons would be released once the search was completed. Thick, black smoke rose around the fairground in almost every direction, the smell overpowered his nostrils and he had to struggle to keep from coughing.

He knew, had known before they arrived, what was happening. He wouldn't say he was looking forward to the mission, but neither was he dreading it. He had a job to do, and he just wanted to get it over with. But everything was done systematically, and there was a lot of standing there, waiting for the next step.

As he waited, machine gun in hand, more and more troops arrived with villagers in tow. The look on their faces told him they were afraid. Understandably so, considering the circumstances.

The whole thing took longer because as the commander of the regiment spoke, a translator was required, so the speech took twice as long as it should have. He stood there and did his best not to let the impatience register on his face.

Once all the people were assured they would all be let go once no weapons were found, it was clear they were relieved. No one seemed to be concerned when some of the troops began to round up the women and children and led them away, though many appeared bewildered by the strategy.

Next, the men were rounded into six groups, and each group was led to a different part of the town. Patton had brought his group to a barn on the west side of the city. The men were told it was merely to keep them out of the way until the search was completed.

Again, they waited.

Then there was the sound of an explosion and immediately after, a gunshot. The two were so close to-gether as to almost be simultaneous.

Once he heard the single gunshot, the other sol-diers with him in the barn began to fire along with Patton. There was no hesitation from any of them. Their orders were clear.

The gunfire roared, and the near fifty villagers in the barn fell almost at once.

Their screams, combined with the soldier's guns, were deafening. Patton wanted nothing more than to cover his ears but was fearful of what might happen if he was found to be insubordinate, so he kept firing until he was sure not a single villager was left standing.

Diekmann's orders had been to shoot for their legs so they would die slowly. He had found this odd but obeyed. This was his life. To obey the orders of his commanding officer without question. And he did it proudly. He did it for the good of his country.

Once the carnage ceased, screams still filled the air, but not as loudly as before since the majority of them had died. Only a few remained alive, but once they saw the gas cans brought in by the soldiers, the noise doubled.

The troops, Patton among them, sprayed the bodies with gasoline and ignited them. The barn went up quickly, and the smell of rotten meat cooking made him want to throw up, but he dared not since he didn't want to appear weak in front of the others. He gazed upon the flames doing his best to appear deadpan.

Once they were finished at the barn, they were or-dered to the church where Patton found more bodies. This time, they belonged to the women and children who had been brought here earlier. Since the corpses were outside the building, he assumed they had been gunned down while trying to escape after an incendiary device had been set off. There had to have been at least a hundred bodies.

Looking back on the incident, he remembered how unemotional he'd been throughout the ordeal. As far as he was concerned, it was another day at the office. He did his job and went home and never lost a wink of sleep over it. Any of it.

They had been told one of their commanding officers had been kidnapped by the French and the slaughter had been their retaliation. Though he was certain the villagers could not have had anything to with the kidnapping, they needed to get their point across that no one could get away with interfering with their plans.

They felt their mission was a success.

"Oradour-sur-Glane," the older man said, letting his mind return to the present.

Belanger nodded.

"Come inside."

The younger man seemed a bit taken aback by the offer, and did not attempt to move.

"Why should I?"

"Well, I'm not sure it's wise for you to be seen standing at my front door with a gun in your hand. Somebody might see you."

"I suppose that's a good point..."

"Not to mention the fact that I assume you would like some answers before you kill me."

"Now that you mention it—"

"On top of all that, I hate being alone in this house and I would like some company."

Belanger followed him into the kitchen without further comment.

"Coffee?"

Belanger nodded and Patton brought him a steaming cup and placed milk and sugar in front of him on the table. Then he sat down across from the man who was trying to choke down the coffee with tears still streaming freely down his cheeks.

"Now," Patton said. "Why exactly have you come here?" He paused for a moment, then added, "I mean other than to kill me."

There were a few moments of silence as the younger man regained his composure.

"First of all, what should I call you? Henry Patton? Or Heinrich Von Paten?"

"Von Paten?" He let the name sink in for a moment. It had been so long since he'd heard it.

"That's not my name anymore." He took blew on the hot coffee then took a sip.

"Why did you kill my father?"

"Well, first of all, it's simply a matter of he was at the wrong place at the wrong time. Secondly, you don't know for sure it was me who killed him. There were lots of soldiers present. There's no evidence that a single person was hit by a bullet from my gun. The men were divided into six groups. He might not even have been at the same barn as I was. He could easily have been among one of the other five groups."

"But you were there."

"Yes, I was."

"You fired into the crowd."

"I did."

"Why?"

"The most obvious answer is that's what I was ordered to and I did."

"Just like that?"

"At the time, we were under the impression that Helmut Kampfe had been captured and was being held there."

"But that wasn't the case?"

"No. We found out two things after the fact. The first being he was rumored to be held at Ouradure-sur-Vayres. Supposedly, a mistake had been made and we went to the wrong village. We also learned he had never really been captured to begin with."

"So, all those people died for nothing?"

"It would appear so."

"And you get to go on living, free of consequences for the part you played in those deaths."

"I wouldn't say that."

"Why not?"

"I have suffered in many ways for what I have done in my past. I continue to suffer this very day. I doubt that would make you feel any better, though."

"It doesn't"

"And shooting me in the head is going to make me suffer? Quite frankly, I'm disappointed you didn't have the balls to do it. I've been waiting for someone to figure out who I am, so they could kill me since I'm too chickenshit to do it myself."

"Let me guess, you want to die because you are ashamed of what you've done and you feel you deserve it."

"No. I want to die to end my suffering."

"What suffering?"

"Let me tell you something, Mister Belanger. There are a total of 642 ghosts in this house. I know that because I am the last one left. Every soldier who was there with me has either been put to death for war crimes or has died of old age, and every ghost from that village has found me. Now that I am the last, they have all come to me."

"Come to you? For what?"

"Why, to torment me, of course."

"You expect me to believe you are haunted by the ghost of every person slain that day?"

"Believe what you like, but let me tell something: I have had cancer for the last 20 years."

"I don't see what bearing that has on anything."

"The doctors told me I only had a few years, at the very most. By all rights, I should be long dead by now."

"What is your point?"

"Don't you see? They're keeping me alive."

"The ghosts?"

"Of course the ghosts! Who else would it be?"

"So, these ghosts are keeping you alive. For what purpose?"

"My God, man! Haven't you been listening? To torture me. They won't let me die as all the rest have. They want me to live on so they can continue to drive me mad. The others are all gone. They have decided to keep me alive so they could continue exacting their revenge on those who they feel wronged them."

"Why you? What makes you so special?"

Patton let out a sigh, shaking his head. "I wish I knew." He lifted his head and looked Belanger in the eyes. "Every day I ask myself, and them, that very question. Why were all the rest allowed to die, but not me?"

"And do they answer?"

He shook his head. "My only theory is perhaps because I am the only one who feels no remorse."

"None at all?"

"I was doing my job. Nothing more. I did what I felt was right at the time."

"And do you still feel it was the right thing to do?"

"Perhaps. I haven't thought about it much."

"How could you not? You slaughtered hundreds of people. How could that knowledge not torment you?"

"I'm sure it would any other man. But I suppose I'm not like other men."

"You aren't helping me to have any sympathy for you."

"I'm not trying to." He eyed the gun. "I've been wondering how long it's going to take you to get the courage to shoot me."

"I'm not waiting for courage. I just want to try to understand you before I kill you."

"Understand me?"

"I wanted to know why you willingly helped slaughter hundreds of people."

"So, now you have your answer."

"I do. But now I'm curious about you. I wonder what kind of monster feels no remorse for something like that."

"The worst kind, I suppose. I've spent fifty years in this very house. My neighbors all regard me as a kind old man. None of them have any clue as to my past. They don't know what I've done, but I'm sure they would be appalled if they knew."

Patton offered the Frenchman a smile. I am the kindly, elderly gentleman next door. But I would kill you without even flinching. Without having to stop to think about it. I am the worst monster there is."

"Yes. You are."

"So, what are you waiting for?" He looked at the gun again, then looked back at Belanger. The younger man still made no move for the weapon. "You'd be doing the world a great service by taking me out of it."

"I'm sure I would. But I intend to make you suffer. Shooting you in the head won't accomplish that."

"But you must do it," Patton insisted. "You must."

Belanger remained motionless.

"Don't you want to avenge your father? I can guarantee he suffered. He was shot in the legs, then burned to death. I'm sure he cried out in pain. Probably cried to God to save him. Cried out to your mother. I wonder if her name was the last thing that came out of her mouth. Or perhaps his last thought was that of his unborn child."

"I know what you're trying to do, but it won't work. You will not anger me enough to shoot you. You say you suffer. Maybe I will leave you to suffer." He paused for a moment, appearing to be in deep thought. "Or maybe," he continued, "I'll do just what you did to those poor people. Shoot you in the legs and burn this house down with you still alive inside it."

"You don't have what it takes to inflict that kind of suffering on someone. You're too good of a person. It takes a certain kind of man to be that cold-hearted. You are not that man."

The Frenchman stood and took his gun from the table and regarded the older man for a long while.

Finally, Patton thought. He's finally going to do it.

But Belanger just shook his head and started walking toward the door.

"Where are you going?" Patton shouted after him. "You can't leave. You have to kill me."

The younger man turned to face him once again. "I've realized that being alone for so many years, with nothing to do but think about the horrendous things you've done has driven you insane. I think by killing you and releasing you from that madness, I would be doing you a favor. Instead, I'm going to leave you here, and let you continue to torture yourself. That's what you deserve."

Again, he turned and walked out of the kitchen.

Patton ran after him and tackled him, both of them hitting the floor with a loud thud. The older man, surprised he still had the agility to pull off such a feat, knew he had the advantage of surprise, but the gun did not fall out of Belanger's hand as he'd hoped. Instead, he still held it tightly as he tried to fight off his attacker.

The German did not expect it when the younger man managed to turn himself around with Patton on top of him, and swung the gun at his head. It reached its target with a satisfying clunk. Patton released his grip and slunk to the floor. Not unconscious, but he went limp, knowing he'd been beaten.

He lay on his back, feeling the blood as it dripped from his forehead down his face, looking at Belanger, silently pleading with him to help him end his life.

"I won't kill you," the Frenchman told him again, then threw the gun at him. It landed on his chest then fell to the floor. "You'll have to do it yourself."

Patton slowly sat up and picked up the gun in his hand. "Thank you," he said softly, raising the weapon to his temple. He pulled the trigger, deafened by the loud bang.

It took him only a second to realize he could smell

gunpowder, and only another second to realize he shouldn't be able to smell anything.

"No," he whispered, tears streaming down his face now. "This isn't right. Why won't they let me die?"

"So, it's true. The ghosts are keeping you alive." There was a look of either shock or awe on the Frenchman's face. The realization brought a smile to Belanger's lips. He turned around and walked out of the house, leaving Patton screaming on the floor of the hallway.

THE END OF THE WAR

It's almost over.

The war between humans and zombies that has raged for as long as I can remember is at its end. The last of them is a mere three feet in front of me, writhing in pain. I can end this now and the world can be at peace.

I take a step toward it and stop. I want to savor the moment, bask in my victory. I shouldn't take pleasure in my enemy's suffering, but I do. We have been murdered relentlessly by these things for years. Even my earliest memories are of survival. Run. Hide. Repeat. We've felt nothing but fear and helplessness as we were hunted and killed without understanding why. Now, it seems, the tables have turned.

The creature struggles to get up, but can't. It wants to get away, struggles to get to its feet but it's at my mercy. I can take as much time to enjoy this as I want.

Another step. It turns its head to look at me. It's afraid. I've only known them to show relentlessness and a lack of mercy. Now I know they feel fear and the revelation is somehow satisfying.

A third step. I'm close enough to look into its eyes

and it looks back at me, ceasing its struggles long enough to use its eyes to plead with me. It can't speak, so it uses facial expressions to beg for mercy.

But I do not intend to show mercy.

I intend to make this thing suffer as its kind has done to us.

I take the final step and I am close enough to end it. But I don't. Not yet. It's not a danger to me. Not anymore. I don't have to worry about it attacking me. Its injuries are too severe.

I crouch down, slow and deliberate. I want it to know its end is coming. I want the realization to sink in and add to its suffering.

I open my mouth and lower my head and, in a satisfying moment, the human race comes to an end.

DEATH WALKS AMONG THEM

THE SMELL OF FRESHLY CUT GRASS, ONE OF MIKE'S favorite scents, wafted in through the window, accompanied by the whirring of a lawnmower outside. With it came the summer heat, which made him almost regret not heeding his wife's pleas for an air conditioner by telling her it would be too expensive. After all, with the advance he'd been promised for the sale of his first novel, they should be able to afford it now. Maybe he'd talk to her about it later. But for now, Mike watched, transfixed on the older man who was pushing the machine up and down the lawn.

"Hey, honey!" he shouted, not bothering to turn away from the window. "You gotta come see this!"

Julie poked her head in from the kitchen, a look of annoyance telling her husband he had interrupted her.

"What is it now?"

"Death's mowing his lawn."

Without even having to look at her, the exasperated sigh told him he should have kept his mouth shut. "Would you leave the poor man alone already? I don't understand why you're so obsessed with him."

"Hey, it's not every day you get to see the grim reaper doing yard work."

He waited for a response and when none came, he turned his attention from the window to the kitchen door, noticing Julie was no longer there. Most likely, it was her subtle way of telling him she had no interest in the activities of the man across the street.

Undaunted, he walked over to the kitchen where Julie was busying herself preparing dinner, the smell of roast and boiling potatoes almost making him forget why he had entered the kitchen in the first place.

Almost.

"I mean, come on," he continued. "Don't you see any humor in this at all?"

Julie gave him one of those looks that should have told him enough was enough. Even Mike was aware of the fact he had not let go of the subject ever since Henry had told him he was the grim reaper. She had told him over and over that the joke had gotten old, but Mike wasn't entirely convinced the older man had been kidding. When he'd first said it, Mike searched for Henry's face for a hint of a smile, or a twinkle in his eye. Something to show he was pulling his leg. But there was no such sign. Henry's expression had been as deadpan as if he'd told Mike he was an accountant.

"He's a very sweet old man," she continued, "and I'm tired of hearing about this. Please just let it go."

"Sweet old man?" Mike almost shouted it. "He's insane. He thinks he's Death."

"Are you stupid?" she finally yelled at him. The words hit like a truck, and he stared at her dazed. "He was joking with you. Nothing more. Now just shut up about it and let's get on with our lives!"

Mike said nothing. Instead, he turned and retreated to the solitude of the bedroom, closing the door behind him. He placated himself by imagining Julie preparing her apology for her harsh words, but he knew no apology was coming. Since they were married, he couldn't recall a single time when she had admitted being wrong in any situation. More often than not, one of them would leave the room and they would remain separated until the next morning when they would pretend nothing ever happened.

Lying on the bed, he looked up at the ceiling, wishing he and Julie hadn't fought. The day had been going well. Since it was Sunday, they stayed in bed later than usual, her head resting on his chest and neither of them saying a word. Just enjoying each other's company.

The rest of the day was spent in quiet relaxation and he'd been hoping it would continue into the evening when they could curl up on the couch together and enjoy a movie, which would most likely lead to something else afterward.

No chance of that now, he thought. All because he was obsessed with that delusional idiot across the street.

Of course, Mike also knew he wouldn't be in this predicament had he not taken the joke too far. Maybe he had been a tad bit obsessive about it.

He thought about apologizing to Julie, but then remembered her "stupid" comment and decided it was her that should be saying she's sorry. Not him.

He rolled over onto his side and let his thoughts carry him to sleep.

Mike didn't wake up again until he felt the covers being pulled off him and then back on as his wife slid into bed. He stayed on his side, keeping his back to her, not letting her know he was awake.

"Are you still mad?" she said in her soft voice, the one she used when she was feeling amorous. But Mike wasn't giving in. He stayed in position, making sure to keep his breathing in a steady rhythm, making it seem like he was still asleep.

"Mike? Are you awake?"

He still said nothing and, after a few more tries, he heard her roll over as well, and before long, she had fallen asleep.

However, he found himself unable to sink back into unconsciousness after having slept away the afternoon. Instead, he stared at the clock, watching the numbers change, getting more frustrated as the morning grew closer. He was fixated on the glowing red numbers, changing rhythmically every sixty seconds.

Just after 2:30 am, Mike was stirred from his trance by the sound of sobbing. He could hear the whimpers in the darkness but he couldn't quite pinpoint from which direction it came.

His first thought was Julie had not fallen asleep and she was more upset about the incident than she'd let on.

He positioned himself so he was facing her and gently placed a hand on her shoulder. But instead of feeling her body shaking in time with the sobs he still heard, it moved up and down, slowly, in perfect time with her breathing.

She was still asleep.

So who was crying? Was it coming from outside?

Mike thought about going to the window to see if anyone was outside, but as he sat up, he could see a figure sitting on the edge of the bed, head held in its hands.

"What the fuck are you doing here?" Mike said, but kept his voice as quiet as he could, not wanting to alarm Julie unless necessary.

"It's all over," the figure said. "It's all over."

Mike squinted, attempting to make out the figure in the darkness. "Henry? Is that you?"

"It doesn't matter how long you live," the figure continued as if it didn't even notice Mike had spoken, "it always seems too short when you learn it's your time to die."

Mike shifted closer to the figure. "Henry? What's going on? What are you talking about?"

"I'm talking about death, Michael. My death."

"Your death? What do you mean?"

"I'm going to die. My time has come."

The only thing Mike could think to do was place a hand on the old man's shoulder, hoping it would offer some form of comfort. Mike never had been very good in social situations.

"What are you talking about? You seem perfectly healthy to me." Mike's idea of death had come from chick flicks Julie had made him watch, so he always imagined it as people slowly wasting away. Having had no one close to him pass away, those movies were the only thing he had to go on.

"It's over," Henry said yet again. "My time has come." He lifted his head and turned to look at Mike. "And you have to take my place."

"Take your place? As what?"

"Death."

The younger man leaped off the bed, distancing himself from his neighbor.

"Okay, this has gone far enough. The joke was funny at first, but come on, enough's enough."

Even Mike was surprised to hear himself say those words, considering how obsessed he'd been about since he'd first met Henry, but even he was getting tired of it by now.

"You thought I was joking?"

"Either that or you've gone off your rocker."

Henry stood, slowly, as if trying to make sure he didn't alarm Mike. He took a step toward the younger man.

"The only reason I told you was that I knew it was you who would replace me. You've been chosen."

"Chosen?"

"Yes. You will leave the life you are living and you will become the Angel of Death in my place. Call it your destiny if that helps you come to terms with it a bit better."

"Why me?"

Mike's received a shrug in response. "I don't know. I don't even know why they picked me. But you're the one."

The younger man shook his head. "This doesn't make any sense."

"Sure it does. I was the Angel of Death. I served this post for three hundred years. Now it's your turn, and you will do it for the same amount of time and then someone else will be chosen."

"Three hundred years?"

Henry nodded.

"There's no way you've lived three hundred years."

"Three hundred and forty, actually. I was forty years old when I was picked."

"You look good for your age." The intention had been to lighten the mood, but he failed miserably.

"I don't think now is the time for jokes."

"Maybe you're right. I think now is the time for a psychiatric hospital. You need help."

"I'm beyond help now. My death is inevitable."

Mike let out a sigh. There was no reasoning with the man. "Alright, let's say I buy into this whole story, how long do I have before I become death?"

"Sunrise."

"Sunrise?"

"Yes. At sunrise, I will die and you will officially take over my position."

"A little clichéd, don't you think?"

"The powers that be can be melodramatic that way. But I'm glad to see you have accepted your fate so readily."

Mike shook his head. "I haven't accepted shit."

"I'm sorry?"

"You think I'm just going to accept this bullshit story of yours and pack up and leave my family? I don't think so. There is no way I'm leaving Julie and the baby. Not to mention my novel is about to be published, and you think I'm just going to give all that up? Now, I'd appreciate it if you left."

Henry moved to the bedroom door but turned around just before exiting.

"I'll be back at sunrise," he said, "and then you will take my place."

Before Mike had a chance to respond, the door closed and he was left trying to figure out if the incident had occurred or if he had dreamed the whole thing.

Maybe he did fall back asleep after all.

Then again, maybe not.

A noise to his left—a rustling of the blankets—surprised him and for the first time since Henry's mysterious appearance, he noticed his wife still in the bed, sound asleep. He rushed over to her side and began to gently shake her.

"Honey, wake up."

"Huh? What?"

"Come on, wake up."

"Oh, not tonight, Mike. I have a headache."

He noticed her begin to drift off again, so he shook her more forcefully."

"Julie! Wake the hell up! We have to go!"

"Go? Go where?"

"Away. Come on, we need to leave now."

She sat up; a lot slower than Mike would have liked, and examined her surroundings.

"Jesus, Mike. It's not even 4 am. What are you thinking?"

"I'm thinking we have to go. Now would you get your ass out of bed?"

He flicked the light switch, the darkness vanishing in an instant, replacing it with a bright light that made Julie have to cover her eyes. Mike then began searching the closets until he found a suitcase, which he then threw on the bed, almost hitting his wife.

As he grabbed clothes from the closet and began stuffing them into the suitcase, not bothering to fold them, Julie's demeanor seemed to change from annoyance to pure pissed off.

"Would you tell me what's going on?"

"Henry's gone nuts."

"Henry? What's he got to do with anything?"

"He was just here?"

"Here? In our room?"

"Yes. Here in our room." He was trying not to be short with her, but time was running short and he needed her to understand the gravity of the situation. "He was going on about him dying and me taking his place and leaving you."

Julie rubbed her eyes and stretched, letting out a yawn in the process. "You're not making any sense."

"Neither was he. The guy is whacked out of his head. I think he might be dangerous. He was going on about death and things like that. Who knows what he might do if he's unhinged?" Mike ripped the covers off her so fast she might have gotten burnt. "Come on, we're getting the hell out of here before he comes back with a hockey mask and a machete."

"I think you're exaggerating."

"You wouldn't think so if you'd been awake for our little midnight chat."

He closed the case and ran out the door, not waiting to see if she was behind him. By the time she made it out to the car, he'd already put the suitcase in the trunk and was waiting in the driver seat with the engine running.

"I still think you're overreacting."

"I don't," was all Mike said before backing the car out of the driveway.

He'd lost track of how long they'd been on the road when she stirred awake.

"Where are we?"

"Exactly where I want to be."

Julie glanced around. "Looks like the middle of nowhere."

"Yup. Someplace nice and isolated."

"He's an old man. How dangerous can he be?"

"I'm not taking any chances." He took his right hand off the steering wheel and placed it on her belly. "Especially with you being pregnant."

"Why couldn't you just call the cops?"

Mike hesitated. What could he say without sounding like a total idiot? Something inside him almost believed Henry. He wasn't sure why, exactly. Maybe it was the sincerity in the old man's voice. He believed himself, and despite not wanting to, Mike thought he did too.

"We'll call them soon. I just figured the best thing was to get you out of there first. I mean; what if he came back before the police could get there."

Her face showed she didn't believe him, but she said nothing more. She closed her eyes as he continued to drive. The green digits on the dashboard clock showed 5:15. It wasn't long until sunrise. Once it passed, Mike could be sure nothing was going to happen and he could call the cops and let them deal with Henry.

He saw a light in the distance. As he grew closer he saw it was a sign for a motel. A small place that looked like there wasn't a single guest spending the night— there was only one car in the lot, and Mike figured it probably belonged to the desk clerk. He pulled in and shut the engine off.

"What's going on? Where are we?" Julie asked, opening her eyes.

"Someplace safe. Wait here while I get us a room."

He walked into the office only to find the clerk snoring in a chair. Apparently, the kid had grown accustomed to the sound of the bell, since it wouldn't wake him up no matter how loud Mike rang it. So, he picked up the register book and slammed it against the counter as hard as he could. The clerk shot out of his chair, startled.

"What the hell, man?

"I'd like a room, please."

"Fine. Forty bucks a night upfront. Sign the register."

Mike signed the book under the name Martin Stillwater and handed over two twenties from his wallet.

"Here, take room one. It's right next to the office."

"Sounds lovely," Mike said, taking the key.

Within five minutes, they had brought the suitcase into the room and Julie was already lying on the bed, trying to get back to sleep.

Mike was contemplating going back to the office to complain about being given a room reeking of stale cigarette smoke and cheap beer when someone knocked at the door.

"Who could that be?" Julie asked, her voice groggy.

"Probably that stupid kid from the front desk. Maybe he's here to give us turn down service."

He swung the door open and his heart lurched inside his chest.

"Hi, Mike!"

"How the fuck did you find us?

"Okay, exactly what part of `Angel of Death' are you not getting?" Henry pushed past Mike and walked into the room. When Julie saw him, she jumped out of the bed.

"What are you doing here?"

"Your husband here has decided to shirk his duty."

"What duty?" she asked.

Henry turned his attention to Mike, shaking his head. "You mean you didn't tell your wife about our discussion? Mike, I'm disappointed in you." He looked back at Julie. "Your husband has been chosen to be my replacement. He's going to be the new grim reaper. It's a promotion. You should be proud."

"Mike was right. You are nuts."

"I wish I was. If so, I wouldn't be dying. But, unfortunately, everything I'm telling you is the truth."

"So now what?" she asked, sitting back down on the bed.

"We hang out until the sun comes up. Then I die, Mike takes my place, and all is right with the world."

"This sounds messed up."

"Well, I'll admit I'm not crazy about the dying part, but we all have to accept our fate. Mike here is having a hard time with that himself. The way I see it, he's getting the better part of the deal if you ask me."

"What do you mean?"

"Only one of us is walking out of here alive." He glanced over at Mike. "Well, somewhat alive."

"How can you be so glib about this?"

"Hey, when you deal with death for as long as I have, you tend to become a little desensitized to it." He let out a long, dragged-out sigh. "Well, unless it's your own, apparently."

He sat down on the bed next to Julie. "I gotta say, even after living for over three hundred years, I still feel like it wasn't enough. I don't want to go yet."

"I can't say I feel sympathy for you." Both Henry and Julie looked up at Mike who had remained silent until that point.

"Are you still feeling sorry for yourself? Geez, you think you're the only one that goes through this? Don't be such an idiot. I had a family once too, you know. You should consider yourself lucky. I bet it's easier having to leave a child you've never met. I had six children. Six! My oldest daughter was fifteen when I was called. Do you think I didn't go kicking and screaming? Do you think I still don't wish I could get that time with them back? I missed their weddings, the births of my grandchildren. Guess when I got to see them again. When they died. So how about you get over yourself and accept your destiny like a man."

"And if I choose not to?"

"At what point did I lead you to believe you had a choice. You were chosen. End of story."

He glanced out the window. "Almost time, Michael. Getting nervous yet?"

"I don't think nervous covers it."

"I bet. I was scared shitless when it happened to me. Of course, I didn't have the luxury of the kindly face you see before you."

"Oh? What did you have?"

There was a flash of light, lasting only a nanosecond. When it was gone, Henry was replaced by a hooded figure holding a sickle. Its face, which wasn't hidden by the hood, was pock-marked and looked as though it had been burnt. The faint smell of brimstones emanated from him.

"This," the hooded figured said in Henry's voice.

"Henry?"

"Like it? Better get used to it. This is your future. Hope you don't plan on getting too many dates though. It's hard to ask a woman out when she's running away screaming." He took another look out the window. "Only a few more minutes to go."

"So how does this work exactly?" Mike was trying to kill time more than anything.

"How does what work?"

"This whole switch thing."

"What's to figure out? I die, you become death. It's pretty simple."

"And then what?"

"And then you're Death. You go off and claim your first soul." Henry hesitated for a moment. "Well, two souls actually."

"You already know who my first victim is?"

"Well, since we don't kill people, we don't call them victims. But yes, I do."

"Care to share that information?"

"Not really."

"You're a big help."

Henry crossed the room, the butt of the sickle tapping against the floor of the room. The carpet muffled it, but Mike still found it creepy.

"I'm not here to help you. I'm here to die. I don't like it any more than you like having to take my place."

Light came in through the window, rising slowly.

"It's time," Henry said. "No more chitchat. It's time for me to go."

It happened faster than Mike even thought possible. One minute the ugly, hooded figure stood before him, the next it was gone and Mike stood in place, now wearing the same hood, the sickle held firmly in his hand.

"Well, they say black is slimming. Maybe this is a good look for me."

Julie looked up and Mike noticed tears streaming down her cheeks. When she finally spoke, her voice cracked. "This isn't funny, Mike. Don't you realize what this means? You're not going to see our baby grow up. This is going to be the last time I'll ever see you."

He nodded. "I know. But I didn't have a choice. If I did, I would have chosen you and the baby. You know that."

"Would you?"

"What do you mean?"

"Would you have chosen us?"

"Why wouldn't I?"

"I don't know... I guess I just got the impression you haven't been very happy lately. I thought you were sticking around for the baby."

"I thought so too. But now I'm not sure. I mean, we've been fighting a lot lately and it's been rough, but I love you. I love you more than I ever thought I could love anyone. I would have chosen you."

Julie nodded. "I believe you."

"Well, I guess I better go. I have it on good authority I need to collect a couple of souls."

"So you know who they are now?"

"Not yet. I just figured I—oh wait, I hear a voice telling me something." Mike stood there, listening. His face dropped with each second he stood there. "Oh my god..." he said finally.

"What? What is it?"

"You."

"What?"

"It's you."

"I don't understand..."

"You're dead. You and the baby."

"Mike, that isn't funny."

"I know it isn't. While I was talking to Henry, at some point the strain was too much for you. You died of an aneurism."

She put her head in her hands, tears coming even faster than before. "Please tell me you're joking."

"I wish I was. Oh god, baby. I'm so sorry. I wish there was something I could do."

"So, I'm already dead?"

Mike nodded.

"That wasn't so bad, I guess. But what about our baby?"

"It died with you."

Mike took his hand out from his robe, a baby girl in his arms.

"Is that our baby?"

"Her soul, yes."

"She's beautiful."

"She looks just like you." They gazed into each other's eyes for a long moment, savoring what they always expected to be the most wonderful moment of their lives, not deaths.

"I guess we should go," Mike said finally. "Come on. I'll take you both up."

They left the motel room, Julie's arm hooked around Mike's, the baby in his other arm. Outside, a stairway leading up to the clouds had materialized.

"Can we walk slowly? I don't want this to end yet."

Mike nodded. "Of course we can. I don't want this to end ever."

WOUNDS

Somewhere on the mountain, a hand reached out of the snow. A few seconds later, a second hand appeared. Both were placed firmly on the ground and the small form pulled itself out of the snow, resting on its knees for a few moments before standing up.

It examined its surroundings. This place seemed somehow familiar, but it didn't know why. It also knew that there was something it was supposed to do, but wasn't sure what.

As it scanned the area, its eyes fell upon a familiar shape at the bottom of the mountain. Again, it had no idea why it recognized it, but it had some inkling it contained bad memories. There was something about this form in the distance that filled it with anger and hatred, but instinct told it to go there, so it began a slow descent down the mountain.

Mary O'Reilly had been staring out the window for most of the day and continued to do so well into the evening. The sun had set so gradually she hadn't even realized it had completely disappeared and night had settled in. Even through the darkness and the flurries of snow, she could still almost make out its form in the distance, almost fifteen miles away. It was easier to make out since the living room was almost in complete darkness itself, lit only by a few candles.

The mountain seemed to be looking back at her, taunting her. There was something evil about it, Mary knew. It mocked her. She pictured it with a face. Eyes that stared at her and a mouth turned up into a malicious grin.

The only time she took her eyes away from the window was when she heard the sound of a glass being set back on the table, and she would glance over at her husband, Bob, to see if he was doing anything other than drinking himself into a stupor.

Of course, he wasn't. He sat in his chair facing the television, which remained off, taking small sips from a glass every few minutes. She would only shake her head at him and turn her attention back to the window.

After a few minutes, she heard him utter a groan and when she turned back in his direction she saw the big man slowly walk into the kitchen, not even bothering to turn on the light. She noticed that he didn't bother to bring the glass with him this time. She found out why when he returned, holding a forty-ounce bottle of Glenfiddich by the neck in his right hand. He had grown tired of going back and forth to the kitchen and had found a solution to the problem.

Mary watched as he sat down and poured another glass. Again, she shook her head. For almost twenty years, this is how they spent January 23rd.

She hated to see him like this. Normally, Bob

wasn't a heavy drinker. A beer or two a day was normally his limit. Some days, he didn't drink at all.

But, as it closer and closer to the twenty-third day of the month, she noticed her husband's mood get steadily worse. She knew, however, come morning, he would be better, and by the end of January, he would be back to his jovial self.

"He'll be coming tonight," she said without looking away from the window.

"Uh-huh."

She waited a moment, hoping that he would at least glance in her direction. Instead, he kept staring at the black screen of the small television set, sipping from his glass.

"So, you're just going to sit there and drink all night?"

"So, you're just going to stand there and stare at that damn mountain all night?" he shot back.

"Well, what do you expect me to do? I'd like to move on, but how can I if you won't?"

He said nothing. He picked up the glass and downed it, then twisted the cap off the bottle and refilled it once more.

It had been snowing lightly when it had begun its trek down the mountain. By the time it had reached the halfway point, a full-blown blizzard had formed. It had trouble making out the shape in the distance through the blistering snow, but instinct told it which way to go. It followed this instinct and continued, not bothered by the storm. It knew it had something to do and, even though it wasn't yet certain what that job was, it would let nothing deter it.

It continued on its way down, knowing its duty must be accomplished before the light came.

"I think we should move back to the city," she said. This time it wasn't just to break the silence, but she felt a desperate need to leave the place they had called home for several years.

She heard a rather loud sigh come from the chair. "Not this again." The words came out almost like a whine. "We've already talked about this."

"Yes, we have, but I don't think I can stay here anymore. I know we moved here for a reason, but that reason is gone. I don't see why we're still here."

"And where do you think we should go?"

"Back to Halifax."

"I like it here. It's quiet and I like my privacy."

"So we'll move to somewhere outside the city, but I want to at least be near it."

"Why? What's the difference?"

"People! That's the difference. Things to do. I mean, we can't even go to the movies here. We have two restaurants to choose from if we want to go out to eat, neither one of them is what I would consider a nice place. I want to be able to go out and do stuff. I feel cooped up in this house. I'm going crazy here. Please, Bob, let's move back."

"Mary, we both agreed to move here."

"Yes, because we didn't want to raise kids in the city. We wanted to move somewhere we thought it would be safer. Well, I don't think that applies anymore."

He downed his drink and filled the glass once more.

"If you fill that glass one more time, I'm going to smash that bottle over your head."

"What is your problem tonight?"

"My problem? I should be asking you the same

question. It's been almost twenty years. I wish you would hurry up and get over this so we can both move on. I think moving back will help us do that."

"Get over it? We're not talking about a pet or something here, Mary. This isn't something you just get over."

"I know it's not. But it's been so long. How long do you want to live like this? You have to learn to forgive yourself. It was an accident."

"Yes, but Jonathan's still dead, isn't he?"

"Yes, he is. But it's not your fault."

"Whose idea was it to go for a hike in the mountains? In the middle of winter, no less. What was I thinking?"

"You were thinking that it would be a nice way to spend time with your son. I let you go. I didn't know how dangerous it would be. It's as much my fault as it is yours." There was a long pause as she waited to let him consider her words. Then she continued, "Maybe we should get counseling."

"I doubt it'll help."

"It couldn't hurt to try."

"Except for the fact we can't afford it."

"I'm sure we can find a way. We have issues that need to be resolved."

"Like what?"

"Like what?" she yelled. "Like the fact that you're letting this eat you up inside? For twenty years! Seriously, Bob, I think you need professional help. You need to realize that Jonathan is dead and it's not your fault. Maybe he died for a reason."

She saw Bob's head peek out from behind the back of the chair. "What reason could there possibly be?"

Mary felt a lump in her throat, making it difficult

for her to express the thoughts she had kept secret from her husband all these years. When the idea had first occurred to her, she was ashamed of herself. But as the years passed, the idea made more and more sense to her.

"I think God took him."

"God?" His astonishment was obvious. "You think God killed our son?"

"Well, you weren't working. We just about lost our home. We could barely afford to feed ourselves, let alone our son. He was suffering. I think God took him to heaven so he wouldn't suffer any more than he already had."

"You've got be kidding."

"Why? I think it makes sense."

"Because if that were the case, why are there so many kids still suffering? Why doesn't God just take them all up to heaven? If anything, it would have been to punish us."

"Punish us for what?"

"For having a baby when we knew there was no way we could afford it. We were being selfish, Mary."

"How can you say that?"

"Because it's true. What right did we have to bring a kid into the world? No job, no money. We were selfish and that's all there is to it." He paused to take another drink. "But the problem's been taken care of now, hasn't it?"

She turned to look at him, shocked. "What's that supposed to mean?"

"Nothing. Just that Jonathan's not suffering anymore."

Mary eyed him suspiciously, knowing there was something he hadn't told her. She decided not to press the matter, however, since she was tired and didn't feel like arguing anymore.

"I'm going to bed," she said. "Are you coming?"

Bob shook his head. "I'm going to stay up and wait."

She knew he would end up drinking until he passed out, as he did every year, but she chose not to try to convince him to give up and come to bed. Experience told her it would be useless. Instead, she climbed the steps leading to the bedroom without another word.

The small figure had finally made it to the bottom of the mountain, and the storm showed no sign of calming. Still, it knew the way. The shape was much closer now—it must be since it had once again become visible through the storm, but it could also feel its hatred growing as it neared the object. It knew it was almost there. It wouldn't be long now.

Bob continued to sit in the chair, not having moved since Mary had gone to bed. The house was completely silent. Most of the candles had gone out by now. Only one remained lit. The bottle beside him was almost empty, but it hadn't done his job. The memories remained. Although, he shouldn't have been surprised. It was the same every year. He drank until he could barely remember his own name, yet the events from that night, so many years before, remained with him.

Guilt and shame invaded him as he remembered everything that had happened.

The discussions between him and Mary came back to him.

He remembered he had suggested putting the boy up for adoption. As far as Mary was concerned, it was out of the question. Jonathan was her son, and no one could love him and care for him as well as she.

So, despite Bob's protests, it was decided that the boy would stay.

It's not that Bob didn't love Jonathan. Quite the opposite. Bob loved him more than anything, which is why he wanted to give his son up for adoption. He had spent eight agonizing years watching him grow up and suffering as he did.

They couldn't afford to feed him properly, which meant the boy was malnourished and weak. With every passing day, Bob hated his wife more and more as he was forced to watch Jonathan go without things he needed. They had even spent a winter with no heat and were forced to wear their winter coats, mitts, and toques all the time, even as they slept.

Even Mary, who had been a healthy weight when she and Bob had first met, had dropped down to under a hundred pounds and Bob, who had been slightly obese, was now at his ideal weight.

He had tried several more times to convince Mary to allow the boy to be adopted by a family capable of taking proper care of him, but Mary was adamant that only she could love him as a mother loved her son.

Finally, Bob could take no more.

He went to refill his glass once more and realized the bottle was empty. He put it back on the table and closed his eyes.

Eventually, his body could keep itself awake no longer. His fatigue combined with the alcohol he had consumed took its toll and he unwittingly drifted into unconsciousness.

———

The small figure had finally reached its destination. It was a small two-story house, and something inside the creature knew it had been there before.

It spent a moment or two gazing at it trying to remember why it had been here in the past and why it was here now.

It opened the door and walked in. Everything was quiet and dark, except for a single candle resting on a table. It found itself mesmerized for a moment by the flickering flame. Then it turned to find a man sitting in the chair, his eyes closed. He just sat there, staring at it. It stared back, trying to remember where he knew the man from.

A feeling of déjà vu came over it.

It seemed to remember being in this room before, looking at this same man as he slept in that exact chair. But the memory wasn't a good one. For whatever reason, its hatred only increased. It didn't take long to realize that its anger was directed toward the man.

Slowly, his eyes opened. The man stared at the creature for a long time, not saying anything. The creature stared back, trying to discern what it was about his man it hated.

Finally, the man spoke to it.

"Mary was right. I don't know how she knew, but

she was right." He shook his head in disbelief. "I wanted to believe it, but I had to be sure."

Still, it said nothing. Just kept staring at the man before him.

"I'm so sorry," he continued. It noticed water coming from the man's eyes at this point and it was now having trouble discerning his words. It had to focus to understand him. "I waited so long just to tell you that."

More water came and the man had an even more difficult time speaking.

"Please understand I only wanted what was best for you."

The creature reached up and felt the back of its head and discovered a sizable hole. It used its finger to feel the inner contour of the hole, causing a memory to come flooding back. It was back on the mountain. The man was there too. It remembered being so happy the man had taken it there. It had wanted them to spend time together. It had run ahead, dragging a sled and laughing as the man walked slowly behind.

When it had stopped and was looking around, he heard the man whisper something. It had sounded like, "Please forgive me, but this is the only way." The next thing it heard was a loud noise. It felt a jolt of pain in the back of its head pushing it forward and into the snow. Next, there was only darkness.

It looked up at the man, who was still crying. Something came to it. "F-f-father?"

The man smiled. "Yes," he said. "I am your father."

There was another long pause and they regarded each other.

"I'm sorry," the man said yet again. "I couldn't take

care of you properly. I couldn't let you suffer, and I didn't know what else to do. Can you ever forgive me?"

It didn't recognize the word "forgive." It looked at this man and felt only anger and hatred. That was all it knew.

The man kept staring at it, not blinking as if waiting for an answer from it, but it didn't know what to say. It may not know what it meant to forgive, but somehow it knew it didn't want to.

Its instinct kicked in once again, and it leaped on the man, knocking the chair and both of them backward. It landed on top of the man.

His eyes gave away his fear, but he didn't struggle. He lay there and let the creature sink its teeth into his throat. Not hard at first, just enough to draw blood.

The man was breathing heavily and whimpering silently, but still didn't struggle. It was as if he felt he deserved to die.

The creature looked into the man's eyes. The fear and hurt in them made it feel something he hadn't in a long time, if ever. Compassion. It had intended to hurt this man as much as it could. Revenge was the only thing it knew up to this point. But seeing this man as it had never seen him before, vulnerable, made it feel sorry for him. It no longer had the urge to torture him.

In one quick movement, it leaned in and tore his throat out in one bite. The man's body went limp and his head thumped back, hitting the floor. Blood poured out of his throat.

The creature knew it had accomplished the task it was meant to. It wiped its mouth and left the house, making its way back up the mountain and knowing it would never come back to this house again.

LITTLE ANGELS

THE WIND CARRIED THE SCENT OF SALTWATER TO WHERE Gary stood. He gazed at the ocean, feeling a mist of water hitting him ever so gently, and thought, *What an amazing place to die.*

It had been years since he was last here and he forgot how beautiful it was. Or maybe he didn't notice the last time, having been so young. Just entering his teen years.

Gary wasn't sure what brought him back to this specific place other than he remembered it being a beautiful and peaceful place. His memory had been right. He couldn't imagine a better place to end his life. He just wished Beth and Anna could share it with him.

But that wasn't possible.

He marveled at the vast body of water before him and his mind, always overthinking everything, drew parallels to his own life. The waves rising and crashing again seemed to mirror his own life in the way that he also only seemed to rise as high as certain outside forces would allow, only to come crashing back down again, leaving him back where he started. Or, more of the case, even further behind. The ocean, seemingly endless in its length, width and depth reminded him how insignificant he truly was in the world, let alone the universe. It also reminded him he was alone. Though, he didn't need to be reminded of that. It smacked him in the face every time he walked through his front door and had to stop himself from calling out to his wife and daughter, reminding him he was alone now.

The shore formed a small bay and to the right, just barely within sight of his peripheral vision, he could make out a small cemetery on a cliff overlooking the water.

How fitting there would be a cemetery in the place where he chose to die. But even what appeared to be a dilapidated old cemetery that hadn't been kept up since the days of Noah and the flood, couldn't detract from the majestic scene.

In a few short days, he would take a swim in that ocean, going out as far as he could until he was too tired to go any further...or swim back.

When he turned around, the image of beauty was spoiled by the row of weather-worn cabins advertised as "rustic" on the website. The years since he had last been there, back when he was a kid, definitely hadn't been kind to them. He remembered the exteriors being a lot nicer, though maybe that was just how he viewed them in his childish excitement.

He almost turned around and found someplace else since the whole point of coming out here was to die someplace beautiful. Someplace that wasn't the shitty apartment he called home for the last year.

Home? It wasn't his home. It was just a place where he slept and watched television.

The only reason he hadn't turned around was he had saved for a year for this trip and he already paid for the whole weekend. Besides, he wasn't planning on dying in the cabin. He intended to let the ocean's current whisk him away and let the water envelop him like a hug from an old friend. Maybe not the most glorious or painless way to die, but in his mind, it was poetic.

When he first entered cabin 6, he was pleasantly surprised. The interior was kept up much better than the exterior had been. It was a small two-bedroom cabin. The living room had enough space for a couch and a small TV. There was a kitchen with about two feet of counter space, one foot on either side of the sink, and a few cupboards. There was also a small table pushed up against one wall with three chairs around it. It didn't seem big enough for a small family, but for him, it was the perfect size. He enjoyed the cozy feeling it permeated. He felt comfortable. Safe, even.

Even walking through the door of the cabin, he caught himself almost calling out to Beth and Anna to let them know he had returned. For one brief, glorious moment, he thought they were on a family vacation.

But there would be no family vacations. Not for them.

He sat on the couch and turned on the TV. He needed something to take his mind off Beth and Anna, or else he would go insane. Even his new surroundings couldn't help take his mind off things, so he hoped some mindless entertainment would. He flipped through a series of reality shows, talk shows, depressing news reports, unable to find anything remotely entertaining. He just kept flipping through, going through all 30 channels more times than he could count before he turned it off and sat staring absentmindedly at the black screen, not realizing the pitiful human being staring back at him was his own reflection.

He stood up, not wanting to spend his last few days on the couch. A glance at the window told Gary dusk was setting in, which happened to be his favorite part of the day. The weather cooled down to just the right temperature, the reddish sky provided enough light to still be outdoors even when there were no streetlamps. He put on a pot of coffee and waited impatiently for it to finish brewing, listening to the sound of it percolating, thinking how repulsive a sound it was.

He poured himself a cup and went outside to light a cigarette. He'd started smoking outside when he and Beth had first moved in together and now found it hard to break the habit.

As he puffed and sipped away while standing on the porch—it was so small it could barely be classified as a porch—his attention again went to the cemetery on the cliff. He stared at it long enough that his curiosity got the better of him. The one thing that got his attention was how small it was. It couldn't have been a public cemetery and there were less than twenty gravestones as far as he could tell. It was almost as if it were a private one, set up for a specific purpose.

Coffee mug in hand, he chucked his butt away, missing the can he'd placed at the door by a few inches, and started to walk up the hill leading to the graveyard.

When he got there, he realized he had made a terrible mistake. He should have known this would happen. Stepping anywhere near a graveyard would bring on thoughts of death and thus bring back memories of departed loved ones.

Gary wasn't prepared for the onslaught of memories of his wife and daughter. Tears rolled down his cheek as he looked at the graves. These kids were taken from this world too soon, but they still had a better shot at life than Anna. She never had the chance to feel safe in her parents' arms, to be kissed on the forehead, to laugh, to take her first steps, say her first word. She never had the chance to know she was loved.

A sound interrupted his thoughts. A rustling in the trees behind him, not quite nearby but not far enough away to call distant.

He turned to look, but the noise stopped as soon as he did.

Wildlife was his first instinct. Surely there were animals in the area. Squirrels, rabbits, maybe even a deer. But he couldn't shake the feeling he was being watched. It made him uneasy, but he dismissed it as paranoia. He turned his attention back to the graves to distract his mind and keep it from working overtime.

The gravestones were crude, obviously done by amateurs. Cut from what looked like cement rather than the marble ones you see nowadays. The tops of them were rough as if whoever had done the cutting had used whatever tool was available at the time and was in too much of a hurry to do the job with care. The place was old and hadn't been kept up over the years. Some of the headstones had been knocked over and left there, lying on the ground. The carvings on them were hard to make out, and Gary had difficulty making out the names on some of them. The ones he could make out, however, unnerved him a bit. Every grave belonged to a child. The oldest one he found was twelve years old.

He had a vague recollection of visiting the place when he was younger. His family had stayed in one of these cabins during one of their many trips to Cape Breton Island since that's where Gary's father had grown up and most of his family had remained. One of the reasons he'd chosen to come to Cod Cove Cottages was the fond memories he had of staying there for a family reunion so many years ago.

He was almost positive he remembered waking up one morning and seeing his father at the graveyard, examining the stones, just as Gary was doing now. When he went up to see what his dad was doing, the man had commented how strange it was that they all belonged to kids but dismissed it as most likely having been some sort of disease that killed them.

Thinking back on that time, it almost made sense to Gary that a disease was the cause of death for these children buried beneath him. The only thing that didn't make sense about the theory was they all died on the same day. September 24, 1911. Even if some sort of plague wiped them all out, it seemed unlikely they would all die on the same day.

Darkness began to settle in and Gary realized there was very little lighting other than the moon and if he stayed any longer, it would be difficult to find his way back so he decided to head to the cabin. Besides, the graveyard in the dusk was starting to creep him out to the point it played with his mind. Gary could swear he heard voices in the surrounding bushes. He couldn't make out what they were saying, but they sounded like the excited whispers of children. He knew this wasn't possible. As far as he knew, there weren't any other people staying in any of the cabins, save for an older couple in the unit next to his own. He'd caught a glimpse of them when he first arrived but didn't say anything. He wasn't out to make friends.

As he drew near, he could see the shape of a man sitting on a chair, illuminated by the porch light hanging above the door.

"Checking out the graveyard, I see," a friendly voice called out as Gary walked closer.

"Yeah. Just thought I'd get some air."

"What'd ya think?"

Gary was close enough to make out an older man sitting in the chair. His right hand held a beer bottle, which he sipped from periodically.

"It's a graveyard. It's old and hasn't been kept up. What else is there to think?"

"Did ya notice the dates?"

"Yeah. They all died on the same day. I thought that was a little odd."

Gary was now close enough to reach out and touch the old guy, so he put out his hand. "Gary Becker."

The man shook it. "Tom Riley."

They sat in silence for a few moments, Tom put his head back, as if the sound of crickets was relaxing him.

"I thought it was weird too," Tom told him. He pointed to a cooler filled with beer bottles, Gary shook his head as he sat down on the extra chair. "I seen that graveyard before but never bothered to check it out. I went up there yesterday, mostly just to get away from the wife for a bit. She gets in a bad mood after a long drive and she was drivin' me up the wall." He let out a chuckle. "I noticed the dates on those stones. Didn't think too much of it, but I happened to run into the lady that runs the place, so I asked her if she knew anything about it."

"And did she?"

"Yup. But I wouldn't advise asking her. She wouldn't shut up about it. She just babbled on with some story about the devil and mutants, or something. Christ, after twenty minutes I had to walk away 'cuz I couldn't make heads or tails out of anything she was saying."

Gary chuckled, more to be polite than anything. He was disappointed that Tom didn't know the story. He'd piqued Gary's curiosity.

"So you don't know much about it then?"

"Not really. Something about how a bunch of kids born around here were deformed. No one knew why. Guess back in those days they didn't know much about science and medicine and such, so no one had any clue why there seemed to be so many kids born with all these deformities. Inbreeding is my guess.

"Anyway, some preacher came by and saw these mutant kids, or whatever you want to call 'em. This preacher must've been one of those fire and brimstone guys 'cuz he convinced the folk that those kids were cursed because of some sin the town had committed. He called them 'Children of the Devil' or some nonsense. Convinced all 'em folks that God was pissed at 'em and there was only one way to make things right."

Gary wasn't sure he wanted to hear the rest of the story. He was starting to see where this was leading. "You don't mean—"

"Yup. They had to kill the devil's spawn. The preacher said it was the only way to save the town from God's wrath, if you can believe that. And, according to the dingbat that owns this place, that's exactly what they did. Mind you, I don't believe a word of it."

Gary wasn't sure if he did. It did seem a bit far-fetched, but the story bothered him nonetheless. Possibly because it made more sense than a bunch of kids dying from some disease all on the same day. He excused himself by saying he was tired and needed sleep. A little white lie, but he was uncomfortable with the way the conversation was going, especially with someone who was a complete stranger not ten minutes ago.

He walked back into the cabin, grateful for the silence for once. He plopped down on the couch and enjoyed a few peaceful moments of blissful nothingness. He liked not having to get up in the morning to go to work. He liked that he had two full days left to enjoy himself and do whatever he wanted before he ended his own life. He liked that during his last moments, he'd have a view of the ocean and die gazing upon the beauty of God's creation instead of the inside of the crappy apartment he moved into after the deaths of Beth and Anna.

After a while, he decided to at least try to get some sleep, even though he wasn't all that tired. He hadn't planned on there not being much to do. He remembered the place being more active the last time he'd been there. Of course, that was more than twenty years ago.

In the darkness of the room, he could make out the outline of a picture he'd placed on the nightstand beside the bed. It was a picture of him and Beth had taken shortly after their wedding. The day she told him about Anna.

The day he found out he was going to be a daddy.

———

"I'm pregnant." It began with those words. Two simple words announced the beginning of life. But indirectly, they also announced the beginning of death, as all life eventually dies.

It's sudden. Alive one minute, gone the next.

But Gary didn't think about death when his wife told him she was pregnant. His mind focused only on the life growing inside her; the life he helped to create. He remembered kissing her, a long and passionate kiss neither of them wanted to break. For the first time since he was a kid, tears streamed down his cheeks. It was the happiest he'd ever been. Probably the happiest he ever would be. He couldn't remember anything that could top that moment.

They broke their embrace, but still held hands, not wanting to let go of each other. Gary was the first to let go, taking out his camera. He wanted to get a picture of Beth to commemorate the moment. But she had a better idea. She snatched the camera out of her husband's hands and ran up to a stranger, thrusting it into the poor unsuspecting man's hands, leading him over so he could get a picture of the happy couple. Rather, the happy family since, technically, there were three of them.

Gary never printed the picture. It stayed on his camera, as most of the pictures did, all but forgotten. It wasn't until afterward when he was scrolling through the images on the digital camera that he found it and remembered the circumstances under which the picture had been taken and he got it printed and framed.

Now, that once-forgotten photograph was his prized possession. The only one he had of his family.

Beth told everyone it was going to be a girl. Gary had no say in the matter. As far as his wife was concerned, there was no doubt their first child would be a daughter. Though whenever Gary questioned her on how she could know so early into the pregnancy, her response was always, "I just know."

Even from the very beginning, from the day she announced while they were enjoying a picnic in the park, she was already referring to the baby as "she."

Though, far be it for Gary to disagree with her at that moment. They were both so excited at the prospect of being parents for the first time, of raising a child together, it seemed like a petty reason to disagree. So he let it go. Then each time after, he let it go again. Either way, the baby's sex couldn't be controlled, so he decided it was best to keep his mouth shut and let it play out.

Besides, Gary was too busy freaking out. As a younger man, he'd been too intent on living his life and could never picture himself as a family man. He had parties to attend, women to sleep with, beer to drink. A family would just get in the way.

Until he met Beth, who swept him off his feet the first time they met and for the first time in his life, he not only pictured himself being with her until the day he shuffled off this mortal coil but longed for it. Craved it.

And now they had created a miracle together. They had created life.

Everything seemed to be going well. As far as the doctor and the ultrasound were concerned, there was absolutely nothing to be concerned about.

So, of course, Gary spent his days off work painting what was going to be the nursery. Pink, of course, since there was no doubt in Beth's mind that it would be a girl. Gary was hoping for a boy, though he never voiced the thought out loud. It had nothing to do with the typical guy thing of wanting a boy to have someone carry on the family name and have someone to teach to throw a football and watch Saturday Night Hockey with. No. He just wanted to see the look on Beth's face when she heard the cry of, "It's a boy!"

Since the first trimester is considered the most dangerous where a woman is most likely to miscarry, once into the second trimester, Beth became even more obsessive. She started stocking up on maternity clothing, even though she wasn't even close to showing yet. Gary found himself building a crib in his spare time. Not putting one together out of a box from Ikea. No way. Gary was told he would be building one from scratch, with his own two hands because it would be a labor of love their child would appreciate for years to come.

This only served to reinforce in Gary's mind that his assumption was correct. Women were insane.

All in all, the happy couple looked forward to the arrival of their little bundle of joy.

Then one night, Gary awoke in the middle of the night. At first, he failed to discern what might have startled him into consciousness. The house was still. Silent.

He sat up in bed for a moment, listening to make sure.

There was a presence in the room. Gary was sure of that. It wasn't like those weird feelings people get in the middle of the night when they think there's a ghost in their room. There was an actual person—or people—in his bedroom. Despite not being able to see any figures moving around in the darkness, his belief that he and Beth were not alone could not be shaken.

He leaned over the side of the bed, feeling around for anything he might be able to use as a weapon. There was nothing, except the small bedside lamp and he would look silly brandishing that at an attacker. Better to die than look silly.

Gary went to get out of bed, shifting his position a little louder than he intended.

"He's awake," came a whisper just loud enough for him to hear, followed by the shuffling of feet on the stairwell.

Gary leaped out of the bed, his spryness surprising even himself, and ran to the stairway to check. He saw no one. He went down to the front door to make sure it was still securely locked. There were no signs of forced entry.

He took a brief tour of the house, making sure nothing seemed out of place, checking all the windows to make sure they were all closed and locked. Nothing was out of place. He returned to the bedroom, feeling foolish having left Beth there by herself. For all he knew, someone could have still been in there with her and who knows what they would have done to her while he was chasing nothing around the house. But when he got there, Beth still lay in the bed sleeping as if nothing had happened. He put his arm around her and tried to go back to sleep, but found he couldn't. Every few seconds, he'd swear he heard a noise and it startled him back into wakefulness only for him to realize his mind was playing tricks on him.

It was at least an hour later when he was able to get back to sleep.

It didn't last long though. Beth woke him shortly after. And not in the way she normally did, which was to gently kiss his neck and gently rub his back. This time, she shook him, hard. He didn't open his eyes at first, his mind was busy trying to process what was happening. The first thought that popped into his head was an earthquake. Gary quickly dismissed the idea when he realized it was some*one* that was shaking him. When his eyes popped open, he noticed Beth. He was about to laugh, thinking she was trying to be funny, but then he noticed the tears in her eyes and the look of pure terror on her face. Then he saw the blood on the sheets and he felt his face turn white.

Gary wasn't an expert in matters concerning pregnancy and childbirth, but he was pretty sure bleeding was a bad sign. He rushed Beth to the emergency room.

Gary hated hospitals under the best of circumstances. Nothing good ever happened in them. It's where people went to die. Every one of his family members who went into a hospital didn't come out until it was time to be transferred to the morgue.

The waiting was the worst part. He sat in the waiting room while the doctors examined Beth. He tried to insist on going in. No doctor was going to tell him to wait outside while his wife and child were in danger. But the doctor threatened to call security and Gary realized he was being more of a hindrance than a help so he reluctantly stayed behind, unable to find anything to occupy his mind except to imagine every worst-case scenario his mind could conjure.

An eternity and three minutes later, the doctor

emerged, walking straight toward him. The man's face was deadpan, with no sign of emotion to indicate to Gary what was going on until the doctor started to speak.

His mind was in such a fog, he barely heard a word the doctor said to him.

"...very sorry for your loss...these things happen... no way of telling the cause...be fine in a day or two..."

The one thing he did remember the doctor telling him was there would be no need for surgery in cases like this. The fetus would expel itself shortly.

Foetus. That very morning it was "the baby" or "our daughter." Suddenly, it wasn't only the child that had died. Its identity died with it and was now known as "the fetus." Gary thought about how strange it was that people could distance themselves from something just by changing its name. "Child" was too personal. "Foetus" meant you got to sleep later that night.

But neither Gary nor Beth got to sleep that night. Or for several nights thereafter. Gary spent the late evening hours consoling his sobbing wife while he wished he could cry with her, but felt the need to at least appear strong for her. If they both lost it, who would be there to keep them together? Gary had to keep control of the situation, no matter how lost he felt.

The late-night crying sessions went on for months. Gary had taken time off work to be with his wife, but he knew he would have to return soon. His employer's patience would only go so far, but Beth's mood was nowhere near improving and he had no idea what the couple was going to do once it was time for him to go back.

And still, they waited for the dreaded day when

the fetus would expel itself from Beth's body, but after several months, that day still hadn't come.

Gary felt they had waited long enough and took Beth back to the hospital to see what could be done. There was no way he could be sure, but he felt there was a possibility carrying a dead child inside of her could be affecting Beth's mood. It was worth a shot, at least.

They arrived at the hospital and this time Gary didn't bother trying to force himself into the room with the doctor and his wife. He already knew from experience what the outcome would be so when the nurse asked him to stay in the waiting room, he obliged and found himself once again feeling alone and helpless.

More waiting.

Gary was told he would have to wait until the doctors were able to remove the child from Beth. It was dead tissue and dead things encourage bacteria, which could cause Beth some serious problems.

Gary braced himself when the doctor came into the waiting room. He'd been bracing himself the entire time he'd been sitting there. But it was futile. He could have spent a million years preparing himself, but it wouldn't have made him ready to hear what the doctor was about to say.

"There's no fetus."

"What do you mean there's no fetus?" This wasn't asked in a tone that expressed concern or curiosity. Gary was downright pissed off and was screaming at the doctor.

"Just that, Mr. Becker. We figure your wife must have expelled the fetus and either didn't notice or didn't tell anyone."

"How does someone not notice they've expelled a fetus? I'm pretty sure that's the kind of thing you fucking notice."

The doctor shrugged.

Gary punched him.

His thoughts were interrupted by what he the door creaking open, followed by the muffled sound of someone trying to close it without being heard. Next came the distinct sound of the latch being put back into place.

He jerked his head up, listening for any other noises. He thought he heard footsteps approaching the bedroom, but he couldn't be sure. If there were, they were very faint.

He thought about getting up to check it out, but his paranoid mind made him hesitate. Were there deranged killers in these parts? You didn't hear much about that kind of thing in Canada, but out here in the middle of nowhere, you never knew what might happen. There could be redneck cannibals living in the woods for all he knew. Hell, Tom could be one of them and the old man's friendliness could have been to Gary at ease and the elderly couple from the cabin next door could be in *his* cabin at that very moment ready to cut his body into strips and use him to bacon for their morning breakfast. This bothered him, but not because he feared death. Nor did it bother him because he feared pain. Some said pain cleansed the soul, though Gary wasn't sure how, but maybe those people were right. No, it bothered him because it would ruin his entire plan for how he wanted to leave this world. If he were to be murdered in his bed by some psychopath, he would be cheated out of the beautiful suicide he had driven through three provinces to accomplish.

Before he could even get a foot on the floor to pull himself out of bed, he saw a figure standing in the doorway. Though the moonlight coming through the window wasn't enough for him to make out the details, he could see the small outline of what appeared to be a child standing in the doorway. It wore a hood so Gary wouldn't have been able to make out its features anyway.

He could feel eyes on him, watching.

"Hey!" he yelled, but the figure didn't answer. "You've got the wrong house."

The child didn't budge and Gary wondered what he would do if it refused to leave. Calling the police would do nothing since they were so far from any city or town there wasn't likely to be any detachment close enough to make it worth their while to come. Not to mention the extra time it would take them to stop laughing once he mentioned it was a kid in his house. Attacking the child wasn't even an option. That was a no-brainer. There was no way Gary couldn't even *think* about hurting a child, let alone go through with it. He wasn't sure if he could even bring himself to pick the kid up and carry it outside if it should come to that.

By its size, he judged it could be a child of eight or nine, which made him wonder what he would be doing out at this hour of the night. Even more confusing was where the kid came from, since Gary was positive other than his own and the one next door, none of the other cabins were occupied. Unless a family happened to show up in the middle of the night and the kid managed to sneak away unnoticed while the parents unloaded. But that was unlikely.

"Where are your parents?"

The figure still stood, unmoving, in the doorway. Its head was cocked to one side, as one might do when studying another person out of curiosity.

Without taking his eyes away from the door, Gary tried to reach over to the lamp on the nightstand to turn it on. While his hand blindly searched for it, it knocked over the picture of him and Beth. It fell to the floor with a mighty crash and he could hear the splinters of glass scatter across the floor.

"Shit!" Gary said under his breath. Distracted, his gaze went to the spot on the floor where the picture fell, but only for a split second. It was enough time for the kid to react. Gary heard the sound of scuffling feet and by the time he managed to reach over and turn the light on, the doorway was empty.

He jumped off the bed, making sure he did so on the side with no glass, and raced to the door, ripping it open with such force he might have pulled it off its hinges. He scanned the darkness but saw no sign of movement. The night was silent.

But there were few places the kid could have gone. Most of the campground was open, leaving only two places for the kid to go. Either hide behind one of the nearby cabins or into the woods. Gary decided the latter was the likelier of the two so he ran back inside long enough to rummage through the drawers to look for a flashlight. He flicked it on to make sure it worked then took off across the field toward the trees.

Since the kid looked young, Gary figured he'd be able to catch up fairly easily, and once in the forest, he hoped the child made enough noise to give away his position. But as he crept through the brush, there was only silence, save for the rustling of leaves in the wind. At first, Gary thought maybe the kid *had* hidden among the cabins after all and was laughing at the older man for having been duped, but then he heard voices coming from somewhere nearby, though it was hard to tell which direction it came from or what they were saying.

The voices were accompanied by laughter and though it sounded childish, in the darkened forest, it sounded malicious to Gary. Like an evil cackle. He shivered, partly from the sound and partly from the cool night breeze.

He stood still for a few moments, listening, trying to pinpoint the direction of the voices. It was no good. As far as he could tell, they were coming from every direction, which made him even more uneasy. It either meant he was surrounded—which was a distinct possibility since he'd made it far enough into the woods, the clearing couldn't be seen with the use of the flashlight—or he was starting to lose his mind. Either way, he decided it was useless to continue searching and he retraced his steps back to his cabin. Not as easy as he thought it would be. He found it easy to get himself turned around and it took him almost an hour to find his way back.

Once in bed, he tried to go back to sleep but his mind wouldn't let him. At first, he kept thinking about the kid who had barged into his home, which made Gary keep an eye on the door and listening for any sounds out of the ordinary.

Once he was able to push the incident out of his mind, he regretted it and wished for it back as it was replaced by more memories of his wife and daughter.

They named her Anna. Referring to their deceased child as "the baby" didn't seem right. Of course, they gave her a girl's name because no amount of debating prowess could convince Beth it might have been a boy. Gary wasn't about to start trying to convince her otherwise now. If she even thought he was about to dispute her on the sex of their child, she would glower at him, as if to say, "Just try it, buddy, and I'll rip your head clean off."

Truly, Beth just wasn't the sweet, gentle, caring person she used to be.

Though Gary agreed one hundred percent with her decision to take an extended vacation from work after the miscarriage, it still shocked him. Beth was never the type of person to take time from work. No matter what.

She never let anything stop her for long. Beth would soldier on in the face of adversity, which no doubt came from graduating from the school of hard knocks.

No part of Beth's life could be said to have been easy.

But the miscarriage took its toll on her in a way Gary had never seen. She developed mood swings. She could seem happy one moment—not ecstatic or anything, just tiny glimmers of happiness once in a while—to downright pissed off, to as depressed as any human can get. Sometimes he would see all three in a matter of minutes.

She could be laughing at a joke he told her one minute, then ripping him a new one the next for an innocent comment, then bawling her eyes out, feeling guilt for being angry with him for no reason.

Though he didn't like to admit it, Gary looked forward to going to work to get a reprieve. He spent his time at home doing his best to support Beth as best he could, and that alone was taxing. He had to watch every word he said because he knew anything could send her into a rage or send her up to the bedroom bawling for hours on end.

Which was why, one morning after he finished a night shift, he decided to stop for breakfast on his way home.

He needed some time to himself. Something he could do where he wasn't scrubbing floors or looking after his wife.

After all, one hour sitting in a restaurant, enjoying a cup of coffee with bacon and eggs, and reading the morning paper for the first time in a month wasn't going to hurt anyone.

The first thing he noticed when he walked through the front door was the eerie silence. It unnerved him. Since he'd started back to work, upon his return every day by the sound of his wife sobbing somewhere in the house. More often than not, he found her in the nursery, which had been left untouched as if they still expected a daughter to be born soon.

The door creaked open, which, due to the variety of noises in the house—music, television, crying—he'd never noticed it do that before. He called out to Beth, softly at first, then raising his voice with each call after. He received no response.

Maybe she went for a walk, he thought. To clear

her mind. But he wasn't able to convince himself and checked every room in the house for any sign of Beth.

Living room, empty. Kitchen, empty. Bathroom, empty. All three bedrooms, empty.

He found himself staring at the basement door. At first, he didn't see the point in bothering to check. There was nothing there except boxes of unneeded items that were stored until such a time they were needed and the laundry facilities. During her depression, the task of laundry had fallen to Gary since his wife could barely get out of bed some days, let alone manage housework.

Still, he needed to check the entire house to make sure.

There was no switch for the basement light. They had to leave the door open to light their way down the stairs, then pull a chain to turn it on.

Even as he walked down the steps, something didn't seem right.

Sometimes in movies, people would get a bad feeling right before something bad happened. Gary always thought that was stupid and unrealistic.

Until he got one of those bad feelings.

Something in his head screamed at him, Don't turn on the light! Just turn around and go back upstairs and pretend everything is fine.

He turned on the light.

The basement was as quiet as the rest of the house. No washer filling with water, no clothes tumbling in the dryer. Nothing.

Until he noticed a creak coming from a corner of the basement behind the stairs.

Don't go over there! Go back upstairs and watch

some TV and keep telling yourself Beth is out for a walk. Nothing to see here.

He heard the creak again.

He walked toward the sound.

Since Gary wasn't expecting to see anything on the ceiling, his eyes were focused on the floor. What he saw confused him at first. A pair of feet, hovering slightly above the ground, swaying.

Then he realized the feet were attached to a pair of legs. Which, in turn, were attached to a torso, which then tapered into a neck with a rope tied around it with the other end tied to the ceiling.

Then everything went blank for a bit.

The next thing Gary remembered was his home being invaded by police, who in addition to asking him a bunch of inane questions repeated some of the same things the doctor had told him when he found out his child had died. But again, he only caught snippets of it.

"...sorry for your loss...terrible tragedy...nothing you could have done..."

Sorry for your loss. Gary almost found those words amusing. Why was the cop apologizing? Why had the doctor? Were they accepting blame?

Gary heard those very words about a million times over the next few days after Beth's suicide. He knew they were meant to be comforting, but he could not be comforted. His entire world had shattered.

First, his deceased child goes missing from its mother's womb. Then his wife kills herself.

During that dreadful day, while the cops were still talking to him, and his wife was still hanging from the rafters in their basement, Gary made his decision to leave this world behind.

The next morning, he woke up and went to step out of bed. Thankfully, just before he put his foot down, he remembered the shattered glass and climbed over to the other side.

He brewed a pot of coffee, waiting impatiently as the liquid seemed to drip into the pot at an infuriatingly slow speed. Then, coffee in hand, he went outside and lit a cigarette.

A woman, whom he assumed to be Tom's wife, was outside, sitting exactly where Tom had been the previous evening.

"Good morning," she called out to him. Gary gave her a polite nod.

"Beautiful day, isn't it?"

"It is," he agreed as he went down the one step leading onto the cabin's porch and headed over to her.

"Hey, can I ask you something?" he asked. Without waiting for a response he went on, "Some kid came into my cabin last night. Do you have any idea who it might be?"

"A kid? Can't think of any. Up until you showed up, Tom and I were the only ones here. Other than that lady who owns the place." She looked around as if she thought the owner might be lurking around the corner, waiting to catch anyone who would dare talk about her behind her back. "She's a little odd, that one. We come here every year, and there are rarely any other people around. The place isn't as busy as it used to be. Seems to have started around the time she took the place over."

"Could it be someone from town? Tom said there was one nearby."

"Tom said that? Are you sure? He knows there isn't any town around here. Used to be, but that was almost a hundred years ago. From what I heard, the villagers all moved away after all those kids died." She nodded her head in the direction of the cemetery.

Gary thanked her for the information and went back into the cabin, not in the mood for idle chit chat at the moment.

Since there was little activity around—Tom and his wife were seldom seen and the owner was nowhere to be found either—Gary spent the day doing his best to relax. He took a swim in the ocean—he'd forgotten how cold it was, but once he was all the way in, he found it relaxing.

He went for a walk up the dirt road as far as he could go until boredom overtook him. He wasn't even sure why he went. He tried to convince himself it was merely for relaxing and to enjoy the scenery, but, deep down, he knew he was hoping Tom's wife had been wrong about there not being a town nearby and wanted to see for himself.

At one point, in the afternoon while having another cigarette, Mrs. Riley invited him to have dinner with them. He tried to politely refuse but she wouldn't hear of it.

So, at about six in the evening, Gary found himself sitting at a small kitchen table almost exactly like the one in his cabin, listening to the bickering of the older couple over the littlest things. It made him wonder if he and Beth—had she lived—would've ended up the same way when old age came creeping on their doorstep.

"So, what brings you to Cod Cove?" Tom asked,

ripping Gary from his thoughts. "Not a lot of folks come out this way anymore."

"My parents took me here once when I was a kid. I needed to get away for a bit, and I remembered liking it here, so I thought I'd give it a try." He glanced out the window next to him. "The place sure has changed since then."

"Bet it has. We started coming here 'bout ten years ago. We liked the fact that no one else comes here. We get some peace and quiet."

"Now that our kids are grown and moved out, it's nice for us to get away," Tom's wife, whom Gary had learned was named Gloria, added. "We didn't get to do that too often when they were young."

"So, needed to get away, huh? From what?" Tom's face went serious, the usual playfulness was nowhere to be found.

"Tom! Don't be rude! It's none of your business."

"Jeezus, woman! Can't a man ask someone a question? He knows he doesn't have to answer if he doesn't want to. Christ! I'm just trying to make conversation here."

Gloria stood up and leaned over the table to take Gary's plate, which had been sitting empty for the last five minutes. As she grabbed hold of the plate, she looked him in the eyes saying, "You don't pay any attention to him. He just has a hard time minding his own business."

"It's okay, really," Gary assured her. Then, to Tom, "Since my wife and daughter aren't around anymore, I just thought I'd take some time off work and get away for a bit. The house seems kind of lonely now. I couldn't stand to be there anymore."

House? his brain said. *What house? Did you move out of that shitty apartment when I wasn't looking?*

"Recently divorced, are ya?" Gloria hit her husband on the shoulder with the back of her hand.

"Would you stop prying into his personal life?"

Again, Gary assured her it wasn't a problem. "No. They passed away. A year ago now."

"Oh. Well, I'm sorry to hear that."

Again with the sorry. A lot of sorry people these days.

"It's okay. I've learned to move on with my life." A lie, but what else was he going to say? *I came out here to kill myself because I can't stand living without my family.*

"Good man. You know, my first wife died too."

"Really?"

"Yeah. Cancer."

Gary noticed Tom's eyes when he said it. A shadow seemed to cross over them.

"But, some things work out for the best. A few years later, I met ol' ball and chain here and I couldn't be happier."

"How long have you been married?"

"30 years," Gloria called out from the kitchen area where she was running water for the dishes.

"Really? Feels like a lot longer," Tom added now that he was safely out of his wife's reach. Then he turned his attention back to Gary, his tone becoming more serious. "Gloria tells me some kid was in your cabin last night."

Gary nodded. "He stood in the bedroom doorway and stared at me. I accidentally knocked over a picture frame and I think that scared him off. He bolted out the door right after."

"Are you sure you're okay?"

"Yeah. Why?"

"Well, there ain't no kids 'round here. Not anymore. Not since—"

"I know. Gloria said something about it early."

"Did you get a look at 'im?"

"No. It was too dark. By the time I turned the light on, he was gone."

"Now, that's just odd."

Dinner was followed by a beer. Which was followed by a few more until Gary had decided he'd had enough conversation for one evening. Darkness was once again settling as he went back to his cabin. He stopped for a smoke before going inside.

As he puffed away, admiring the way the moonlight reflected off the water, he could swear he heard whispers coming from behind the cabin.

"Hello?" he called. "Is someone there?"

Just as expected, there was no response.

He walked to the rear of the cabin, finding no one. It could have been his imagination, but he thought he heard something scurry away before he got there.

Maybe there are some kids here that Tom and Gloria don't know about, he thought. But then, wouldn't they know if one of the other cabins had been rented? Surely there would be signs of other people around. A car or something. Plus, they would see other people coming and going from one of the other cabins.

There was something weird going on.

He went into the cabin and decided to attempt to watch a bit of TV before going to bed. But first, he needed to use the washroom after all the beer Tom had given him.

As he was relieving himself, he heard the door creak open. He was sure that's what he heard.

He quickly zipped himself back up and came out of the washroom to see what was going on.

There was no one there.

He walked over to the door, grabbed it by the knob, and shook it. It was closed tightly.

Maybe it was just the wind.

He heard scuttling behind him, but as he spun on his foot and faced the other way, he was still looking at nothing at all.

Your nerves are shot, pal, he thought. *This whole suicide thing has got you rattled pretty good, huh? That's because you know there's no way in hell you're going to go through with it. You're going leave here, chalking it up as a decent vacation, then you're going back to that hell hole apartment and your shitty job and live the rest of your life wondering why in the hell you didn't end it when you had the chance.*

Another noise from somewhere in the house, but he couldn't tell where.

The door he could dismiss as the wind. The scuttling, paranoia. But the loud crashing sound he'd just heard couldn't be explained away. Something was *definitely* going on.

Gary ran to the window and brushed the curtain to the side. Several small figures stood there. Though they were difficult to make out, he could tell each of them was deformed in some way. Though each deformity was unique.

They weren't trying to get into the house, as far as Gary could tell. They were surrounding it. There had to be at least twenty of them, encircling the house.

How the hell can Tom and Gloria not see this? he wondered. *Why aren't they doing anything about it?*

He ran to the kitchen and grabbed one of the

knives he'd brought, facing the door in case one of those kids tried to come in, then realized he hadn't even bothered to lock it.

He moved cautiously to the door, not wanting anyone outside to know what he was doing. He turned the deadbolt until he heard the satisfying "click" of it locking into place, making him feel at least eighty percent safer. If he had any wood handy, he would board up the windows to complete the job.

"I think it's a little late for that," said a voice behind. "You know, considering we're already in the house."

He turned around to find two more deformed kids. Well, three, since one of them was holding a baby, wrapped in an old, brown blanket. Even from where he stood, Gary could see the thing was torn in several places as if it was the only thing they had to keep the poor child warm. It probably was.

"What the hell are you doing here?"

"See? I told you he could see us," said one of them. This one's hair grew in patches on random parts of his head, so he had several bald spots. Also, one eye was higher than the other, making his face seem lopsided. When he spoke, Gary could see his tooth. "He saw me last night when I was here.

"Of course I can see you," Gary said. He was pointing the knife at the two boys, not trying to seem menacing, but at least letting them know he meant business.

"Not everyone can," said the other boy, the one holding the baby. "Only certain people can see us." This one was a hunchback, who only had one eye. Not in the center of his forehead, like a cyclops, but skin covered the area where his left eye should have been.

"What are you talking about?"

"You can only see us if we want you to. If we think you're special enough."

Gary lowered the knife a little, mostly because it felt wrong to threaten kids with it. The older one, with the baby, couldn't have been older than twelve. "So why me? What makes me so special?"

The boy looked down at the infant in his arms. "She does."

"She?"

"She wanted to see you."

The knife lowered the rest of the way down to his side, and fell out of his hand, hitting the floor with a loud clang that left a ringing in his ears. "I...I don't understand."

The boy advanced, holding the baby out to him. Gary took a step back, still unsure if he could trust him.

"Please. She wants to see you."

Gary looked at the boys, then down to the bundle in the older one's arms, his mind trying to fit the pieces together. "No. It can't be...Anna?"

"Is that her name? We called her Emily since we didn't know her real name." The boy offered him a sad smile. "Emily was my mother's name."

Gary raised the knife again, pointing right at the older boy. "This is some kind of trick. That can't be..." He couldn't bring himself to say, think it even. He knew the child couldn't be his daughter, but there was a part of him that wanted—*needed*—it to be true.

"How is this possible?"

"We had to take her. To protect her."

"Protect her from what?"

"The world." The boy looked down at her again,

smiling. "She's like us. She would have been treated like an animal, just like we were."

"I'm her father. I would have protected her."

The boy shook his head. "How? You could only have done so much. You can't keep her safe from the world forever. We can." He advanced again, still holding the baby out to Gary, who, once within reach, moved the blanket away from Anna's face. He shouted and jumped back.

"What the hell is that thing?"

Sadness showed in the boy's eyes. "See? This is why she needs to be protected. Even you, her father, can't love her for who she is, because you judge what she looks like, not what's in her heart. She's a very special girl, you know. She loves you so much. She's why we came here. She wanted to see you.

Gary couldn't believe what he saw was his daughter. He didn't want to believe it. At first glimpse, it looked like a normal fetus. Of course, what was he expecting? It—*back to calling her an "it", are we?*—died at only twelve weeks old. But then he noticed the growth on its neck, forcing its head to cock slightly to one side. Then when he saw its teeth—*teeth? Did twelve-week-old fetuses even have teeth?*—he lurched back, slamming himself up against a wall, with nowhere else to go.

"Please, at least hold her. Just for a minute."

Gary hesitated, but in the end, he found he could not refuse his daughter her request, though how these kids could know what a dead infant wanted, was beyond him. He reached out his arms and allowed the boy to place the bundle in them. He looked down at Anna again. The creature inside the blanket turned its head and opened its eyes to look back at him.

Though this monstrosity startled him at first, he thought he could detect Beth's image in there somewhere. But it could have been wishful thinking. He had said from the moment he found out she was pregnant he had hoped it would look like her.

The child smiled at him. It seemed to recognize him as her dad, though he had no idea how. She had never laid eyes on him until that moment. Maybe it's true what they said, babies know their parents by instinct. Though he thought that only applied to mothers.

Gary touched Anna's face with his finger, rubbing her cheek gently. She grabbed hold of it with her tiny hand but wasn't quite able to wrap her fingers around it. Caught up in the moment, he leaned in to kiss her cheek, but as he came in close, her teeth bared and, before he could pull away, bit down on his nose, somehow managing to fit it all in her mouth.

Gary screamed and tried to drop the child, but the grip on his nose was too tight and the creature wouldn't let go, it just kept increasing the pressure and the pain kept growing until it reached pure agony.

"Don't fight it," the boy said. "Please, let her do what she needs to do."

He tried to speak but he was in too much pain to utter a word. He grabbed hold of the creature and pulled, trying to get it off of him, and he could feel the tearing of skin as his nose came off with it.

He dropped the child onto the floor and he went down as well, pulled his shirt up to his face, to where his nose used to be, putting pressure on it to stop the bleeding.

Tears welled in his eyes, and he saw a blurry version of the boy pick up the creature, who, though just a baby, wasn't crying after having been dropped to the floor.

"Don't you see?" the boy said. "She made you like us." He stood up, cradling Anna in his arms. "Now when you finish what you came here to do, you can join us and be with Anna forever. She wants you to be with her. With us."

With that, the two boys walked out the front door, bringing Anna with them. Just before leaving entirely, the older boy turned back and said, "We'll see you soon."

Gary heard the door slam shut. Using a nearby table, he managed to pull himself up. Still holding his shirt to his face, he stumbled to the window and looked out. He could see a crowd of figures walking through the darkness toward the cemetery.

He glanced back to the floor where the knife had landed. He stared at it for a long moment, trying to decide what he wanted to do. He could do what he had originally planned and spend eternity living with that monstrosity or he could live out the rest of his life with his new deformation, enduring the stares and whispers of those around him.

He walked over to the knife and picked it up with his free hand, then walked into the bathroom, closing the door behind him.

In the Hands of an Angry God

If I had a favorite of my stories, this would be it. I got the idea when I found an anthology looking for stories with silence as the theme. This story came to me and I wrote it quickly. The problem was, I wasn't happy with it. There was something about the story that didn't sit right with me, but I couldn't quite put my finger on it. So, I let it sit. I didn't submit it to the anthology for which I'd written it. It sat on my hard drive for a good two years or so. Maybe longer. Then one day, it hit me. I knew what was wrong with the story. There was an action scene in it that ruined the pacing of the story. This was meant to be an atmospheric tale, and the rather violent action sequence destroyed the atmosphere completely. I deleted the offending scene and I loved the result. Now, I just need somewhere to submit it.

Fast forward another year or so. Craig Spector (if you don't recognize the name, do you even horror, bro?) who co-wrote a few of my favorite books with John

Skipp in the 80s and 90s, was looking for a story for an anthology he was editing. The theme was freedom of speech. I thought this story fit the bill, so I sent it out, assuming it would get rejected. I mean, it's Craig Spector. I had to figure he was getting submissions from some top-notch authors and I didn't have a chance.

It had to be the fastest turnaround I've ever had on a story. If memory serves, I got an acceptance from Craig the next day. The story ended up in the anthology Freedom of Screech, featuring the likes of Chet Williamson, Elizabeth Massie, Jack Ketchum, Richard Christian Matheson, Thomas F. Monteleone, and a host of other talented authors.

So, yeah. I was pretty darn proud of this one.

Terror Eyes

This was an early story. I wrote in 2010, one year after my first story was published. This one made it into eFiction Magazine. If I remember correctly, I think it was for their October/Halloween issue. As for the story itself, I don't remember all the circumstances surrounding the inspiration for it. I do remember an incident that would have taken place around 2004 when my daughter said she saw a man in her room. I remember my wife (now ex-wife) was out somewhere and, from what I recall, I managed to get her back to sleep pretty quickly. That memory stayed in the back of my mind for years afterward and, eventually, it became the basis for this story.

Quality of Life

This story has the distinction of being my first invitation to an anthology, rather than me just submitting it. Many years ago, I belonged to a writers' group. The name escapes me now. It was Wormwood something or other. I'm still in touch with the other four members in one way or another. Back in late 2010 or early 2011, I was contacted by one of the former members of our group, Thom Erb. He was putting together an anthology of zombie stories and wanted one from me. I put my thinking cap on, and I wish I could tell you where the idea for this story came from, but it just popped into my head, almost fully formed, which doesn't happen often with me. I wrote the story and Thom put it in Death Be Not Proud. I was surprised when I saw the list of authors who also had stories in this anthology: Gord Rollo, Jonathan Maberry, Joe, McKinney, Rick Hautala, Lucy Snyder, and (believe it or not) Dave Brockie, also known as Oderus Urungus from GWAR. This story also has the distinction of being the only story I've written that my mother has read.

Fear Itself

This is the oldest story in this book. It was my second published story. The first is a story I have made sure will never see the light of day. I don't write much flash fiction. It's difficult to write a story and develop characters in a thousand words or less. But when I became aware of this market, I decided to give it a try. The editor of the e-zine liked the story and published it. They took it down when I asked them to so I could include it in this collection. The story itself came out of my interest in phobias. Back in high school, a friend of mine had learned of some interesting ones that he shared with me. Fear of jello always stayed with me for some reason, so I put it in the story. I found the tale to be a bit intense, so I thought a little bit of comedy would lighten the mood a bit.

Yesterday's Sins

The idea of a kidnapped angel came from a John Carpenter episode of Masters of Horror called Cigarette Burns. I took that one concept and the idea grew from there. I've always loved this story. I still think it's one of my best in concept, if not execution. This is was my second anthology appearance. Ty Schwamberger picked it up for Dark Things II. Fun fact: Two of the members of the writing group I mentioned earlier also had stories in that book.

Ancestors

This was the first story I wrote specifically for this collection. There was no specific inspiration for the story, I just sat down and started to write and let the story take me where it wanted to go. Having no preconceived notions as to what the story was about, I think it's pretty good.

Monster

Another previously unpublished story. I have a morbid personality, so sometimes I find myself thinking about why people do evil things. So, when I got the idea for a story about a descendant of someone killed by Nazis during the Second World War showing up at the killer's house, I couldn't pass it up. The supernatural elements came to me as I wrote it. I wanted to make sure I got all the details right and I think this is the most research I've ever done for a short story. I still love this little tale and I hope you did too.

Death Walks Among Them

I mentioned earlier I don't write much flash fiction. The exception to this is I have submitted a few flash fiction pieces to Crystal Lake Publishing's monthly flash fiction contest. Five or six, as of this writing. None of my stories have won the contest but this, my first entry, was selected to appear in Crystal Lake's anthology Shallow Waters Vol. 2. This is a huge deal for me as Crystal Lake is on my bucket list of publishers and I see this as a first step to achieving that goal.

Death Walks Among Them

Several years ago, Nancy Kilpatrick was editing an anthology. Instead of just sending the story, as is usually the case with calls for submissions for an anthology, one of the requirements was to send Nancy a synopsis of the story. If approved, you would then write and send the story. So, I wrote the synopsis for Death Walks Among Them and it was approved. Unfortunately, I didn't get the story finished by the deadline, so I'll never know if Nancy would have bought it or not. Still, I've always liked this story. I see is a bit of a morbid love story.

Wounds

This wasn't my first story acceptance. It was my third. But it was my first story that appeared in an actual book rather than just online, so this story will always have a place in my heart for that reason alone. One thing that has always bothered me about this tale is that more than a few readers have referred to it as a vampire story. It is not. The boy in the story is not, nor was he ever intended to be, a vampire. I originally wrote this story for Michael Knost, an editor who has edited several anthologies, but who has not yet bought one of my stories. He's been my white whale, so to speak. If Mike ever does another anthology, I'll try yet again. The particular anthology for which I wrote the story, had an Appalachian theme. So it had to take place around the Appalachian Mountains. This is why this story takes place in Nova Scotia. The mountain chain runs through the province and it happens to be a province I've grown up loving. My father was raised there and I spent many summers there visiting my grandparents as a kid. Mike didn't buy the story but it found a place in Masters of Horror: The Anthology, which was put together by Lee Pletzers.

Little Angels

Speaking of spending summers in Nova Scotia, this story was inspired by one of our visits to Cape Breton Island when I was in my early teens. Our family on my father's side (aunts, uncles, cousins) had rented cabins right on the coast of the Atlantic Ocean. The front door of the cabin was within fifty feet of the water. It was a beautiful spot. When facing the water, off to the left, there was a cliff that overlooked the ocean. One morning, I saw my dad up there looking around, so I went up to see what he was doing. It was an old gravesite, many of the headstones were wooden crosses. When I read the inscriptions, I noticed not a single person buried there lived past the age of twelve. Fast forward to around 2013 or 2014, and that makeshift graveyard was still in the back of my mind. I wondered who those kids were and how they died. The result of those ponderings is this story. I originally published it as a standalone story and got a beautiful cover done by William Cook. It was available for six years and then I took it down to include it in this collection. The original story was reviewed by Renier Palland, who commented, "If a young Wes Craven and David Lynch had a baby, we'd call him Joseph Mulak." That remains my all-time favorite quote about my work.

Dear reader,

We hope you enjoyed reading *Haunted Whispers*. Please take a moment to leave a review, even if it's a short one. Your opinion is important to us.

Discover more books by Joseph Mulak at https://www. nextchapter.pub/authors/joseph-mulak

Want to know when one of our books is free or discounted? Join the newsletter at http:// eepurl.com/bqqB3H

Best regards,
Joseph Mulak and the Next Chapter Team

ABOUT THE AUTHOR

Joseph Mulak is the author of Ashes to Ashes and Haunted Whispers, as well as several short stories. His work has appeared in nearly twenty anthologies and e-zines. He lives in North Bay, Ontario with his wife Alicia. He has five children. You can find out more about him as well as sign up for his newsletter at https://www.josephmulak.com/

Dear reader,

Thank you for taking the time to read *Haunted Whispers*. If you enjoyed it, please consider telling your friends or posting a short review. Word of mouth is an author's best friend and is much appreciated.

Haunted Whispers
ISBN: 978-4-86752-368-1
Mass Market

Published by
Next Chapter
1-60-20 Minami-Otsuka
170-0005 Toshima-Ku, Tokyo
+818035793528

26th July 2021

www.ingramcontent.com/pod-product-compliance
Lightning Source LLC
LaVergne TN
LVHW031432170726
843492LV00010B/2968